MUSIC USE NOTE

Licensees are solely responsible for obtaining formal written permission from copyright owners to use copyrighted music in the performance of this play and are strongly cautioned to do so. If no such permission is obtained by the licensee, then the licensee must use only original music that the licensee owns and controls. Licensees are solely responsible and liable for all music clearances and shall indemnify the copyright owners of the play(s) and their licensing agent, Samuel French, against any costs, expenses, losses and liabilities arising from the use of music by licensees. Please contact the appropriate music licensing authority in your territory for the rights to any incidental music.

RENTAL MATERIALS

An orchestration consisting of **Conductor/Rehearsal Piano Score, Reed 1 (Piccolo, Clarinet, Soprano & Alto Saxophones), Reed 2 (Piccolo, Clarinet, Bass Clarinet, Soprano & Tenor Saxophones) Reed 3 (Clarinet, Bass Clarinet, Soprano, Tenor & Baritone Saxophones) Trumpets 1 & 2, Trombone 1, Trombone 2, Tuba/Bass, Percussion (Glockenspiel, Gong, Drums) Violin, Banjo, Keyboard 1 (Piano, Harmonium), Keyboard 2 (Piano, Accordion)**, and **20 Principal Chorus Books** will be loaned two months prior to the production ONLY on the receipt of the Licensing Fee quoted for all performances, the rental fee and a refundable deposit. Please contact Samuel French for perusal of the music materials as well as a performance license application.

IMPORTANT BILLING AND CREDIT REQUIREMENTS

If you have obtained performance rights to this title, please refer to your licensing agreement for important billing and credit requirements.

ACT ONE

ACT TWO

Chicago

The Musical

Book by Fred Ebb and Bob Fosse
Music by John Kander
Lyrics by Fred Ebb

Script Adaptation by David Thompson

Based on the Play *Chicago* by
Maurine Dallas Watkins

A SAMUEL FRENCH ACTING EDITION

SAMUEL FRENCH

FOUNDED 1830

SAMUELFRENCH.COM
SAMUELFRENCH-LONDON.CO.UK

ISBN 978-0-573-70052-1

www.SamuelFrench.com
www.SamuelFrench-London.co.uk

FORTY-SIXTH STREET THEATRE

ROBERT FRYER and JAMES CRESSON
PRESENT

GWEN VERDON CHITA RIVERA
AND
JERRY ORBACH

IN

A Musical Vaudeville

PRODUCED IN ASSOCIATION WITH
MARTIN RICHARDS
JOSEPH HARRIS and IRA BERNSTEIN

BOOK BY   MUSIC BY   LYRICS BY
FRED EBB and BOB FOSSE JOHN KANDER FRED EBB

BASED ON THE PLAY "CHICAGO" BY MAURINE DALLAS WATKINS

WITH
BARNEY MARTIN   MARY McCARTY   M. O'HAUGHEY

CANDY BROWN   CHRISTOPHER CHADMAN   CHERYL CLARK
GRACIELA DANIELE   GENE FOOTE   GARY GENDELL
RICHARD KORTHAZE   MICHON PEACOCK   CHARLENE RYAN
RON SCHWINN   PAUL SOLEN   PAMELA SOUSA
MICHAEL VITA

SETTINGS BY   COSTUMES BY   LIGHTING BY
TONY WALTON   PATRICIA ZIPPRODT   JULES FISHER

MUSICAL DIRECTOR   DANCE MUSIC ARRANGED BY
STANLEY LEBOWSKY   PETER HOWARD
ORCHESTRATIONS BY   SOUND DESIGN BY
RALPH BURNS   ABE JACOB

HAIR STYLES BY ROMAINE GREEN

DIRECTED AND CHOREOGRAPHED BY
BOB FOSSE

CHARACTERS

VELMA KELLY
ROXIE HART
BILLY FLYNN
MATRON "MAMA" MORTON
MARY SUNSHINE
AMOS HART

The Ensemble/Men
COURT CLERK (Ensemble Member #1)
JUDGE (Ensemble Member #2)
SERGEANT FOGARTY (Ensemble Member #4)
AARON (Ensemble Member #5)
MARTIN HARRISON (Ensemble Member #6)
HARRY/JUROR (Ensemble Member #7)
FRED CASELY (Ensemble Member #11)

The Ensemble/Women
MONA (Ensemble Member #3)
GO-TO-HELL KITTY (Ensemble Member #8)
ANNIE (Ensemble Member #9)
JUNE (Ensemble Member #10)
HUNYAK (Ensemble Member #12)
LIZ (Ensemble Member #13)

SETTING

Chicago, Illinois

TIME

The late 1920s

MUSICAL NUMBERS

ACT ONE

Overture

Scene One
"And All That Jazz" .... **VELMA** and **ENSEMBLE**

Scene Two – The Bedroom
"Funny Honey"..................................... **ROXIE**

Scene Three – The Jail
"Cell Block Tango"................ **VELMA** and **ENSEMBLE WOMEN**

Scene Four – The Jail
"When You're Good to Mama" .... **MATRON "MAMA" MORTON**

Scene Five – The Jail

Scene Six – The Visitor's Area
Scene Seven
"All I Care About" .... **BILLY FLYNN** and **ENSEMBLE WOMEN**

Scene Eight – Billy's Office
"A Little Bit of Good" .... **MARY SUNSHINE**
"We Both Reach for the Gun"....... **BILLY, ROXIE, MARY SUNSHINE** and **ENSEMBLE**

Scene Nine
"Roxie" .... **ROXIE** and **ENSEMBLE MEN**

Scene Ten – The Jail
"I Can't Do It Alone"................................ **VELMA**

Scene Eleven – The Jail
"My Own Best Friend"...................... **ROXIE** and **VELMA**

ACT TWO

Entr'acte

Scene One – The Jail
"I Know a Girl"..................................... **VELMA**
"Me and My Baby" .... **ROXIE** and **ENSEMBLE MEN**
"Mister Cellophane"...................................**AMOS**

Scene Two – The Jail
"When Velma Takes the Stand" .... **VELMA** and **ENSEMBLE MEN**

Scene Three – The Courthouse

Scene Four – The Courthouse
"Razzle Dazzle"......................... **BILLY** and **ENSEMBLE**

Scene Five – The Courtroom

Scene Six – The Jail
"Class"................... **VELMA** and **MATRON "MAMA" MORTON**

Scene Seven – The Courtroom
"Courtroom Sequence"............................**ENSEMBLE**

Scene Eight – The Courtroom
"Nowadays"............................... **ROXIE** and **VELMA**
"Finale"... **COMPANY**

ACT ONE

Scene One

(SCENE: Chicago, Illinois. The late '20's.)

ENSEMBLE MEMBER #1. Welcome. Ladies and Gentlemen, you are about to see a story of murder, greed, corruption, violence, exploitation, adultery and treachery – all those things we all hold near and dear to our hearts. Thank you.

[MUSIC: No. 1 – "OVERTURE"]

*(Following the overture, **VELMA** enters.)*

[SONG: No. 2 – "AND ALL THAT JAZZ"]

VELMA.

COME ON, BABE,
WHY DON'T WE PAINT THE TOWN,
AND ALL THAT JAZZ?

I'M GONNA ROUGE MY KNEES
AND ROLL MY STOCKINGS DOWN,
AND ALL THAT JAZZ.

START THE CAR,
I KNOW A WHOOPEE SPOT,
WHERE THE GIN IS COLD
BUT THE PIANO'S HOT.

IT'S JUST A NOISY HALL
WHERE THERE'S A NIGHTLY BRAWL
AND ALL THAT JAZZ.

SLICK YOUR HAIR
AND WEAR YOUR BUCKLE SHOES
AND ALL THAT JAZZ.

VELMA. *(cont.)*
I HEAR THAT FATHER DIP
IS GONNA BLOW THE BLUES
AND ALL THAT JAZZ!

HOLD ON, HON,
WE'RE GONNA BUNNY HUG.
I BOUGHT SOME ASPIRIN
DOWN AT UNITED DRUG

IN CASE YOU SHAKE APART
AND WANT A BRAND NEW START
TO DO THAT –

VELMA/ENSEMBLE.
JAZZ.

ENSEMBLE MEMBER #2. Skiddoo!

VELMA.
AND ALL THAT JAZZ.

ENSEMBLE MEMBER #1. Hotcha!

ENSEMBLE MEMBER #3. Whoopee!

VELMA.
AND ALL THAT JAZZ.

ENSEMBLE. *(whispered)* Hah! Hah! Hah!

VELMA.
IT'S JUST A NOISY HALL
WHERE THERE'S A NIGHTLY BRAWL
AND

VELMA/ENSEMBLE.
ALL THAT JAZZ.

*(**FRED CASELY** and **ROXIE HART** enter.)*

FRED. Listen, uh, your husband ain't home, is he?

VELMA. No, her husband is not at home.

*(**ENSEMBLE** laughs.)*

VELMA.
FIND A FLASK,
WE'RE PLAYING FAST AND LOOSE.

ENSEMBLE.

AND ALL THAT JAZZ.

VELMA.

RIGHT UP HERE
IS WHERE I STORE THE JUICE

ENSEMBLE.

AND ALL THAT JAZZ.

VELMA.   **ENSEMBLE.**

COME ON, BABE,   WAH, WAH, WAH, ETC.
WE'RE GONNA BRUSH THE SKY,
I BETCHA LUCKY LINDY
NEVER FLEW SO HIGH,

'CAUSE IN THE STRATOSPHERE,
HOW COULD HE LEND AN EAR
TO ALL THAT JAZZ?

ENSEMBLE.

OH, YOU'RE GONNA SEE
YOUR SHEBA SHIMMY SHAKE.

VELMA.

AND ALL THAT JAZZ.

ENSEMBLE.

OH, SHE'S GONNA SHIMMY
TILL HER GARTERS BREAK.

VELMA.

AND ALL THAT JAZZ.

ENSEMBLE.

SHOW HER WHERE TO PARK HER GIRDLE.
OH, HER MOTHER'S BLOOD'D CURDLE
IF SHE'D HEAR
HER BABY'S QUEER
FOR

VELMA & ENSEMBLE.

ALL THAT JAZZ.

FRED. *(to* **ROXIE***)* Come here!

(The "action" between **ROXIE** *and* **FRED** *is very
mechanical.)*

VELMA.	ENSEMBLE.
ALL THAT JAZZ.	OH, YOU'RE GONNA SEE
COME ON, BABE, WHY DON'T WE PAINT THE TOWN,	YOUR SHEBA SHIMMY SHAKE.
AND ALL THAT JAZZ?	AND ALL THAT JAZZ.
I'M GONNA ROUGE MY KNEES	OH SHE'S GONNA SHIMMY
AND ROLL MY STOCKINGS DOWN,	TILL HER GARTERS BREAK.
AND ALL THAT JAZZ.	AND ALL THAT JAZZ.
START THE CAR,	SHOW HER WHERE TO PARK HER GIRDLE.
I KNOW A WHOOPEE SPOT,	OH, HER MOTHER'S BLOOD'D
WHERE THE GIN IS COLD	CURDLE
BUT THE PIANO'S HOT.	
IT'S JUST A NOISY HALL WHERE THERE'S A NIGHTLY BRAWL	IF SHE'D HEAR
AND ALL THAT –	HER BABY'S QUEER
	FOR ALL THAT –

ROXIE. So that's final, huh, Fred?

FRED. Yeah, I'm afraid so, Roxie.

ROXIE. Oh, Fred...

ENSEMBLE WOMEN. Oh, Fred...

FRED. Yeah?

ROXIE. Nobody walks out on me.

*(**ROXIE** shoots him.)*

FRED. But sweetheart –

*(**ROXIE** shoots him again.)*

ROXIE. Don't "sweetheart" me, you son-of-a-bitch!

FRED. Roxie, please –

*(**ROXIE** shoots him again.)*

ENSEMBLE MEMBER #2. Whoopee!

ENSEMBLE MEMBER #3. Hotcha!

ENSEMBLE MEMBER #4. Jazz!

*(**FRED** dies.)*

ROXIE. Oh, I gotta pee.

*(**ROXIE** exits.)*

VELMA.
> NO, I'M NO ONE'S WIFE,
> BUT OH, I LOVE MY LIFE
> AND ALL THAT JAZZ!

ENSEMBLE. *(loud whisper)*
> THAT JAZZ!

Scene Two

(The bedroom. Three hours later.)

AMOS. So I, ah, took the gun, Officer, and I shot him.

FOGARTY. I see, and your wife, Roxie Hart, was in no way involved. Is that right?

AMOS. That's right, Officer.

FOGARTY. Aren't you the cheerful little murderer.

AMOS. Murderer? Why just last week, the jury thanked a man for shooting a burglar.

[SONG: No. 3 – "FUNNY HONEY"]

FOGARTY. Well, that's just fine. Sign right here, Mr. Hart.

AMOS. Freely and gladly. Freely and gladly.

CONDUCTOR. For her first number, Miss Roxie Hart would like to sing a song of love and devotion dedicated to her dear husband, Amos.

ROXIE.

SOMETIMES I'M RIGHT.
SOMETIMES I'M WRONG.
BUT HE DOESN'T CARE.
HE'LL STRING ALONG.
HE LOVES ME SO,
THAT FUNNY HONEY OF MINE.

SOMETIMES I'M DOWN,
AND SOMETIMES I'M UP,
BUT HE FOLLOWS 'ROUND
LIKE SOME DROOPY-EYED PUP.
HE LOVES ME SO,
THAT FUNNY HONEY OF MINE.

HE AIN'T NO SHEIK.
THAT'S NO GREAT PHYSIQUE.
AND LORD KNOWS HE AIN'T GOT THE SMARTS.

BUT LOOK AT THAT SOUL!
I TELL YA, THAT WHOLE
IS A WHOLE LOT GREATER THAN
THE SUM OF HIS PARTS.

ROXIE. (*cont.*)

> AND IF YOU KNEW HIM LIKE ME
> I KNOW YOU'D AGREE.
>
> WHAT IF THE WORLD
> SLANDERED MY NAME?
> WHY, HE'D BE RIGHT THERE,
> TAKING THE BLAME.
> HE LOVES ME SO,
> AND IT ALL SUITS ME FINE,
> THAT FUNNY, SUNNY, HONEY
> HUBBY OF MINE.

AMOS. A man got a right to protect his home and his loved ones, right?

FOGARTY. Of course, he has.

AMOS. Well, I come in from the garage, Officer, and I see him coming through the window. With my wife Roxanne there, sleepin'. Like an angel...an angel!

ROXIE.

> HE LOVES ME SO,
> THAT FUNNY HONEY OF MINE.

AMOS. I mean supposin', just supposin', he had violated her or somethin'...you know what I mean...violated?

FOGARTY. I know what you mean.

AMOS. ...or somethin'. Think how terrible that would have been. Good thing I got home from work on time, I'm tellin' ya that! I say I'm tellin' ya that!

ROXIE.

> HE LOVES ME SO,
> THAT FUNNY HONEY OF MINE.

FOGARTY. (*looking through his wallet*) Fred Casely.

AMOS. Fred Casely. How could he be a burglar? My wife knows him! He sold us our furniture!

ROXIE.

> LORD KNOWS
> HE AIN'T GOT THE SMARTS.

AMOS. She lied to me. She told me he was a burglar.

FOGARTY. You mean he was dead when you got home?

AMOS. She had him covered with a sheet and she's tellin' me that cock and bull story about this burglar, and *I* ought to say I did it 'cause *I* was sure to get off. Burglar, huh!

ROXIE.	AMOS.
NOW HE'S SHOT OFF HIS TRAP, I CAN'T STAND THAT SAP!	And I believed her! That cheap little tramp.
LOOK AT HIM GO, RATTIN' ON ME. WITH JUST ONE MORE BRAIN WHAT A HALF-WIT HE'D BE.	So, she was two-timing me, huh? Well, she can just swing for all I care. Boy, I'm down at the garage, working my butt off, four-
IF THEY STRING ME UP I'LL KNOW, I'LL KNOW WHO BROUGHT THE TWINE.	teen hours a day, and she's up there, munchin' on Goddamn bon-bons and jazzing. This time she pushed me too far.
THAT SCUMMY, CRUMMY DUMMY HUBBY OF MINE.	That little chiseler. Boy, what a sap I was!

ROXIE. You double-crosser! You said you'd stick! You god-damn disloyal husband.

(to **FOGARTY***)* You wanna know what really happened? I shot him. Put that down in your book, palsy. And you wanna know why? He was tryin' to walk out on me.

FOGARTY. That's a pretty cold-blooded murder, Mrs. Hart. They're liable to hang you for that one.

ROXIE. Hang me?

FOGARTY. Not so tough anymore, are you?

ROXIE. Amos, did you hear what he said?

*(***AMOS*** exits.)*

Son-of-a-bitch...Hail Mary full of grace...

*(***ROXIE*** continues to ad lib prayers as ***FOGARTY*** takes her away.)*

Scene Three

(The jail.)

[SONG: No. 4 – "CELL BLOCK TANGO"]

FRED CASELY. And now, the six merry murderesses of the Cook County Jail in their rendition of The Cell Block Tango.

LIZ.

POP.

ANNIE.

SIX.

JUNE.

SQUISH.

HUNYAK.

UH UH.

VELMA.

CICERO.

MONA.

LIPSCHITZ.

LIZ.

POP.

ANNIE.

SIX.

JUNE.

SQUISH.

HUNYAK.

UH UH.

VELMA.

CICERO.

MONA.

LIPSCHITZ.

LIZ.

POP.

ANNIE.

SIX.

JUNE.

SQUISH.

HUNYAK.

UH UH.

VELMA.

CICERO.

MONA.

LIPSCHITZ.

LIZ.

POP.

ANNIE.

SIX.

JUNE.

SQUISH.

HUNYAK.

UH UH.

VELMA.

CICERO.

MONA.

LIPSCHITZ.

ALL.

HE HAD IT COMIN'.

HE HAD IT COMIN'.

HE ONLY HAD HIMSELF TO BLAME.

IF YOU'D HAVE BEEN THERE,

IF YOU'D HAVE SEEN IT,

VELMA.

I'LL BETCHA YOU WOULD HAVE DONE THE SAME.

LIZ.

POP.

ANNIE.

SIX.

JUNE.

SQUISH.

HUNYAK.

UH UH.

VELMA.

CICERO.

MONA.

LIPSCHITZ.

WOMEN.

HE HAD IT COMIN'.
HE HAD IT COMIN'.
HE ONLY HAD HIMSELF TO
    BLAME.
IF YOU'D HAVE BEEN THERE,
IF YOU'D HAVE SEEN IT,
I BETCHA YOU WOULD HAVE
    DONE THE SAME.
HE HAD IT COMIN'.
HE HAD IT COMIN'.
HE ONLY HAD HIMSELF TO
    BLAME.
IF YOU'D HAVE BEEN THERE,
IF YOU'D HAVE SEEN IT,
I'LL BETCHA YOU WOULD HAVE
DONE –

LIZ.

You know how people have these little habits that get you down. Like Bernie. Bernie liked to chew gum. No, not chew. Pop.

Well, I came home this one day and I am really irritated and looking for a little sympathy and there's Bernie layin' on the couch, drinkin' a beer and chewin'. No, not chewin'. Poppin. So I said to him, I said, "Bernie, you pop that gum one more time..." And he did.

So I took the shotgun off the wall and I fired two warning shots. Into his head.

ALL.

HE HAD IT COMIN'.
HE HAD IT COMIN'.
HE ONLY HAD HIMSELF TO BLAME.
IF YOU'D HAVE BEEN THERE,
IF YOU'D HAVE HEARD IT,
I'LL BETCHA YOU WOULD HAVE DONE THE SAME.

WOMEN.

HE HAD IT COMIN'.
HE HAD IT COMIN'.
HE ONLY HAD HIMSELF TO
    BLAME.
IF YOU'D HAVE BEEN THERE,
IF YOU'D HAVE HEARD IT,
I'LL BETCHA YOU WOULD HAVE
    DONE THE SAME.
HE HAD IT COMIN',

ANNIE.

I met Ezekiel Young from Salt Lake City about two years ago and he told me he was single and we hit it off right away.

So, we started living together. He'd go to work. He'd come home. I'd mix him a drink. We'd have dinner. Well, it was like heaven in two and a half rooms.

WOMEN. *(cont.)*

> HE HAD IT COMIN'.
> HE ONLY HAD HIMSELF TO
>   BLAME.
> IF YOU'D HAVE BEEN THERE,
> IF YOU'D HAVE HEARD IT,
> I'LL BETCHA YOU WOULD HAVE
>   DONE THE SAME.
> HE HAD IT COMIN' –

ALL. Hah!

LIZ/ANNIE/JUNE/MONA.

> HE HAD IT COMIN'.
> HE HAD IT COMIN'.
> HE TOOK A FLOWER IN ITS PRIME.
> AND THEN HE USED IT,
> AND HE ABUSED IT.
> IT WAS A MURDER BUT NOT A
>   CRIME.

WOMEN.

> POP.
> SIX.
> U-UH.
> CICERO.
> LIPSCHITZ. ETC.

ANNIE. *(cont.)*

> And then I found out. "Single?" he told me. Single my ass. Not only was he married. Oh no! He had six wives. One of those Mormons, you know. So that night, when he came home, I mixed him his drink as usual.
>
> You know, some guys just can't hold their arsenic.

VELMA/HUNYAK.

> POP, SIX, SQUISH, U-UH, CICERO LIPSCHITZ, ETC.

JUNE.

> Now, I'm standing in the kitchen, carvin' up the chicken for dinner, minding my own business and in storms my husband Wilbur in a jealous rage. "You been screwin' the milkman!" he says. He was crazy and kept screamin', "You been screwing the milkman." And then he ran into my knife. He ran into my knife ten times.

ALL.

> IF YOU'D HAVE BEEN THERE,
> IF YOU'D HAVE SEEN IT,
> I'LL BETCHA YOU WOULD HAVE DONE THE SAME.

HUNYAK. Mit keresek, en itt? Azt mondjok, hogy a hires lakem lefogta a ferjemet en meg lecsaptam a fejet. De nem igaz, en artatlan vagyok. Nem tudom mert mondja Uncle Sam hogy en tettem. Probaltam a rendorsegen megmagyarazni de nem ertettek meg....

JUNE. But did you do it?

HUNYAK. UH UH, not guilty!

WOMEN.

HE HAD IT COMIN'.
HE HAD IT COMIN'.
HE ONLY HAD HIMSELF TO
    BLAME.
IF YOU'D HAVE BEEN THERE,
IF YOU'D HAVE SEEN IT,
I'LL BETCHA YOU WOULD HAVE
    DONE THE SAME.
HE HAD IT COMIN'.
HE HAD IT COMIN'.
HE ONLY HAD HIMSELF TO
    BLAME.
IF YOU'D HAVE BEEN THERE,
IF YOU'D HAVE SEEN IT,
I'LL BETCHA YOU WOULD HAVE
    DONE THE SAME.
HE HAD IT –

VELMA.

My sister, Veronica and I did this double act and my husband, Charlie, traveled around with us. Now, for the last number in our act, we did these twenty acrobatic tricks in a row – one, two, three, four, five – splits, spread eagles, flip-flops, back flips, one right aver the other. Well this one night we were in Cicero, the three of us, sittin' up in a hotel room, boozin' and havin' a few laughs and we ran out of ice, so I went out to get some. I come back, open the door and there's Veronica and Charlie doing Number Seventeen – the spread eagle. Well, I was I such a state of shock, I completely blacked out. I can't remember a thing. It wasn't until later, when I was washing the blood off my hands I even knew they were dead.

VELMA.

THEY HAD IT COMIN'.
THEY HAD IT COMIN'.
THEY HAD IT COMIN' ALL ALONG.
I DIDN'T DO IT,
BUT IF I'D DONE IT,
HOW COULD YOU TELL ME THAT I WAS WRONG?

WOMEN.

THEY HAD IT COMIN'.
THEY HAD IT COMIN'.
THEY TOOK A FLOWER IN IT'S
    PRIME.
AND THEN THEY USED IT,
AND THEY ABUSED IT.
IT WAS A MURDER
BUT NOT A CRIME.

HE HAD IT COMIN'.
HE HAD IT COMIN'.
HE ONLY HAD HIMSELF TO
    BLAME.

IF YOU'D HAVE BEEN THERE,
IF YOU'D HAVE SEEN IT,
I'LL BETCHA YOU WOULD HAVE
    DONE THE SAME.

VELMA.

THEY HAD IT COMIN'.
THEY HAD IT COMIN'.
THEY HAD IT COMIN' ALL
ALONG.
I DIDN'T DO IT,
BUT IF I DID IT,
HOW COULD YOU TELL ME
THAT I WAS WRONG?

MONA.

I loved Alvin Lipschitz more than I can possibly say. He was a real artistic guy. Sensitive. A painter. But he was troubled. He was always trying to find himself. He'd go out every night looking for himself and on the way he found Ruth, Gladys, Rosemary... and Irving. I guess you can say we broke up because of artistic differences. He saw himself as alive. And I saw him dead.

ALL.

THE DIRTY BUM, BUM, BUM, BUM.
THE DIRTY BUM, BUM, BUM, BUM.

LIZ/ANNIE/MONA.

THEY HAD IT COMIN'.
THEY HAD IT COMIN'.
THEY HAD IT COMIN' ALL
    ALONG.
'CAUSE IF THEY USED US,
AND THEY ABUSED US,
HOW COULD YOU TELL US
THAT WE WERE WRONG?

VELMA/JUNE. (**HUNYAK** *babbles.*)

THEY HAD IT COMIN'.
THEY HAD IT COMIN'.
THEY HAD IT COMIN' ALL
ALONG.
'CAUSE IF THEY USED US,
AND THEY ABUSED US,
HOW COULD YOU TELL US
THAT WE WERE WRONG?

LIZ/ANNIE/MONA.	**VELMA/JUNE.** (**HUNYAK** *babbles.*)
HE HAD IT COMIN'.	HE HAD IT COMIN'.
HE HAD IT COMIN'.	HE HAD IT COMIN'.
HE ONLY HAD HIMSELF TO	HE ONLY HAD HIMSELF TO
BLAME.	BLAME.
IF YOU'D HAVE BEEN THERE,	IF YOU'D HAVE BEEN THERE,
IF YOU'D HAVE SEEN IT,	IF YOU'D HAVE SEEN IT,
I'LL BETCHA YOU WOULD	I'LL BETCHA YOU WOULD
HAVE DONE THE SAME.	HAVE DONE THE SAME.

LIZ. You pop that gum one more time!

ANNIE. Single my ass.

JUNE. Ten times!

HUNYAK. Miert csukott Uncle Sam bortonbe.

VELMA. Number Seventeen – the spread eagle.

MONA. Artistic differences.

ALL.

I'LL BETCHA YOU WOULD HAVE DONE THE SAME!

Scene Four

(The jail.)

ENSEMBLE MEMBER #5. And now, Ladies and Gentlemen –
the Keeper of the Keys, the Countess of the Clink, the
Mistress of Murderer's row – Matron "Mama" Morton!

[SONG: No. 5 – "WHEN YOU'RE GOOD TO MAMA"]

MATRON.

ASK ANY OF THE CHICKIES IN MY PEN.
THEY'LL TELL YOU I'M THE BIGGEST MOTHER HEN.
I LOVE THEM ALL AND ALL OF THEM LOVE ME,
BECAUSE THE SYSTEM WORKS,
THE SYSTEM CALLED "RECIPROCITY"!

GOT A LITTLE MOTTO,
ALWAYS SEES ME THROUGH.
WHEN YOU'RE GOOD TO MAMA,
MAMA'S GOOD TO YOU.

THERE'S A LOT OF FAVORS
I'M PREPARED TO DO.
YOU DO ONE FOR MAMA,
SHE'LL DO ONE FOR YOU.

THEY SAY THAT LIFE IS "TIT FOR TAT"
AND THAT'S THE WAY I LIVE.
SO, I DESERVE A LOT OF "TAT"
FOR WHAT I'VE GOT TO GIVE.

DON'T YOU KNOW THAT THIS HAND
WASHES THAT ONE, TOO.
WHEN YOU'RE GOOD TO MAMA,
MAMA'S GOOD TO YOU.

(VELMA enters.)

VELMA. Look at this, Mama. *The Tribune* calls me the "Crime
of the Year." And *The News* says…"Not in memory do
we recall so fiendish and horrible a double homicide."

MATRON. Ah, Baby, you can't buy that kind of publicity. You took care of Mama and Mama took care of you. I talked to Flynn. He set your trial date for March the 5th. March 7th you'll be acquitted. And March 8th – do you know what Mama's gonna do for you? She's gonna start you on a vaudeville tour.

VELMA. I been on a lot of vaudeville tours. What kind of dough are we talking about?

MATRON. Well, I been talkin' to the boys at William Morris and due to your recent sensational activities I can get you twenty-five hundred.

VELMA. Twenty-five hundred! The most me and Veronica made was three-fifty.

MATRON. That was before Cicero, before Billy Flynn, and before Mama.

VELMA. Mama, I always wanted to play Big Jim Colosimo's. Could you get me that?

MATRON. Big Jim's! Well, that's another story. That might take another phone call.

VELMA. And how much would that phone call cost?

MATRON. You know how I feel about you. You're like family. I'll do it for 50 bucks.

VELMA. Fifty bucks for a phone call. You must get a lot of wrong numbers, Mama.

(**VELMA** *exits.*)

MATRON.

IF YOU WANT MY GRAVY,
PEPPER MY RAGOUT,
SPICE IT UP FOR MAMA,
SHE'LL GET HOT FOR YOU.

WHEN THEY PASS THE BASKET
FOLKS CONTRIBUTE TO,
YOU PUT IN FOR MAMA.
SHE'LL PUT OUT FOR YOU.

MATRON. *(cont.)*

> THE FOLKS ATOP THE LADDER
> ARE THE ONES THE WORLD ADORES.
> SO BOOST ME UP MY LADDER, KID,
> AND I'LL BOOST YOU UP YOURS.
>
> LET'S ALL STROKE TOGETHER
> LIKE THE PRINCETON CREW.
> WHEN YOU'RE STROKIN' MAMA,
> MAMA'S STROKIN' YOU.
>
> SO WHAT'S THE ONE CONCLUSION
> I CAN BRING THIS NUMBER TO?
> WHEN YOU'RE GOOD TO MAMA,
> MAMA'S GOOD TO YOU.

Scene Five

(The jail.)

VELMA. *(to* **ROXIE***)* Hey you! Get out of my chair!

ROXIE. Who the hell do you think you are –

MATRON. Roxie, Roxie, this here is Velma Kelly.

ROXIE. Velma Kelly? THE Velma Kelly? Oh, gosh! I read about you in the papers all the time. Miss Kelly, could I ask you somethin'?

VELMA. What.

ROXIE. The Assistant District Attorney, Mr. Harrison, said what I done was a hanging case and he's prepared to ask the maximum penalty. I sure would appreciate some advice.

VELMA. Look, I don't give no advice. And I don't take no advice. You're a perfect stranger to me and let's keep it that way.

ROXIE. Thanks a lot.

VELMA. You're welcome.

MATRON. Roxie, relax. In this town, murder is a form of entertainment. Besides, in forty-seven years, Cook County ain't never hung a woman yet. So it's forty-seven to one, they won't hang you.

VELMA. There's always a first.

MATRON. Tell me, Roxie – what do you figure on using for grounds? What are you gonna tell the Jury?

ROXIE. I guess I'll just tell them the truth.

VELMA. Tellin' a jury the truth! That's really stupid.

ROXIE. Jesus, Mary and Joseph, what am I going to do?

VELMA. You're talking to the wrong people.

MATRON. You see, dearie, it's this way. Murder is like divorce. The reason don't count. It's the grounds. Temporary insanity. Self-defense.

ROXIE. Yeah what's your grounds?

VELMA. My grounds are that I didn't do it.

ROXIE. So, who did?

VELMA. Well, I'm sure I don't know. I passed out completely. Only I'm sure I didn't do it. I've the tenderest heart in the world. Don't I, Mama?

MATRON. You bet your ass you have, Velma.

ROXIE. Is being drunk grounds?

VELMA. Just ask your lawyer.

ROXIE. I ain't got a lawyer.

VELMA. Well, as they say in Southampton...you are shit out of luck, my dear.

(**VELMA** *exits.*)

ROXIE. So that's Velma Kelly.

MATRON. Ain't she somethin'. She wears nothing but Black Narcissus Perfume and never makes her own bed. I take care of that for her.

ROXIE. You make her bed?

MATRON. Well, not exactly. You see, Velma pays me five bucks a week, then I give the Hungarian fifty cents and she does it. Hey, Katalin Hunyak, szeretnem ha megismerned Roxie Hart ot.

HUNYAK. Not guilty.

MATRON. That's all she ever says. Anyway, you know who's defending Velma, don't ya?

ROXIE. Who?

MATRON. Mr. Billy Flynn! Best criminal lawyer in all Chicago, that's who.

ROXIE. How do you get Billy Flynn?

MATRON. First you give me a hundred dollars, then I make a phone call.

ROXIE. I see, and how much does he get?

MATRON. Five thousand dollars.

ROXIE. Five thousand dollars!

MATRON. I'd be happy to make that phone call for you, dearie.

[MUSIC: No. 6 – "TAP DANCE" underscoring]

ROXIE. Five thousand dollars! Now, where in hell am I gonna get five thousand dollars?!

Scene Six

(The Visitors' Area)

ENSEMBLE MEMBER #1. Ladies and gentlemen, a tap-dance.

ROXIE. Oh, Amos, I knew you'd come. I've been sinful – but I want to make up to you for what I done. And I will, just as soon as I get out of here. And I can, too. You see, there's this lawyer, and he costs five thousand dollars.

AMOS. Roxie, I'm tired of your fancy footwork. The answer is "no."

ROXIE. I know I lied to you. I know I've cheated on you. I've even stolen money from your pants pockets while you were sleepin'.

AMOS. You did?

ROXIE. But I never stopped loving you, not my Amos – so manly and so attractive…so…I'm embarrassed…so sexy.

AMOS. But five thousand bucks!

ROXIE. It's my hour of need for chrissakes!

AMOS. Well, okay. I'll get it for you, Roxie. I'll get it.

Scene Seven

[SONG: No. 7 – "ALL I CARE ABOUT"]

ENSEMBLE MEMBER #6. Ladies and gentlemen, presenting the Silver Tongued Prince of the Courtroom – the one, the only Mr. Billy Flynn.

ENSEMBLE WOMEN.

WE WANT BILLY.
WHERE IS BILLY?
GIVE US BILLY.
WE WANT BILLY.
"B" – "I" – DOUBLE "L" – "Y"
WE'RE ALL HIS.
HE'S OUR KIND OF A GUY,
AND OOH, WHAT LUCK,
'CAUSE HERE HE IS!

*(***BILLY FLYNN*** enters.)*

BILLY. Is everybody, here? Is everybody ready? Hit it!

I DON'T CARE ABOUT EXPENSIVE THINGS,
CASHMERE COATS, DIAMOND RINGS,
DON'T MEAN A THING,
ALL I CARE ABOUT IS LOVE.

ENSEMBLE WOMEN/BILLY.

THAT'S WHAT HE'S (I'M) HERE FOR.

BILLY.

I DON'T CARE FOR WEARIN' SILK CRAVATS,
RUBY STUDS, SATIN SPATS,
DON'T MEAN A THING,
ALL I CARE ABOUT IS LOVE.

ENSEMBLE WOMEN.

ALL HE CARES ABOUT IS LOVE.

BILLY.

GIVE ME TWO EYES OF BLUE
SOFTLY SAYIN'

ENSEMBLE WOMEN.

"I NEED YOU"

BILLY.

LET ME SEE HER STANDIN' THERE
AND HONEST, MISTER, I'M A MILLIONAIRE.
I DON'T CARE FOR ANY FINE ATTIRE
VANDERBILT MIGHT ADMIRE.
NO, NO, NOT ME,
ALL I CARE ABOUT IS LOVE.

ENSEMBLE WOMEN.

ALL HE CARES ABOUT IS LOVE.
(OOO)

BILLY. Maybe you think I'm talking about physical love. Well, I'm not. Not just physical love. There's other kinds of love. Like love of justice. Love of legal procedure. Love of lending a hand to someone who really needs you. Love of your fellow man. That's the kind of love I'm talking about. *(rim shot)* And physical love ain't so bad either.

(**BILLY/ENSEMBLE WOMEN** *whistle to…*)

BILLY.

IT MAY SOUND ODD,
ALL I CARE ABOUT IS LOVE.

ENSEMBLE WOMEN.

THAT'S WHAT HE'S HERE FOR.

BILLY. *(ad-lib, Bing Crosby crooning)*

HONEST TO GOD,
ALL I CARE ABOUT IS LOVE.

ENSEMBLE WOMEN.

ALL HE CARES ABOUT IS LOVE.

BILLY.

SHOW ME LONG RAVEN HAIR
FLOWIN' DOWN ABOUT TO THERE.
LET ME SEE HER RUNNING FREE,

(spoken)

Keep your money, that's enough for me!

BILLY. *(cont.)*

I DON'T CARE FOR DRIVIN' PACKARD CARS,
SMOKIN' LONG, BUCK CIGARS.
NO, NO, NOT ME,
ALL I CARE ABOUT IS

BILLY.   **ENSEMBLE WOMEN.**

DOIN' THE GUY IN,   AHH
WHO'S PICKIN' ON YOU.   OOO
TWISTIN' THE WRIST   MMM
THAT'S TURNIN' THE SCREW.

BILLY/ENSEMBLE WOMEN.

ALL I (HE) CARE(S) ABOUT IS LOVE.

Scene Eight

(Billy's office.)

BILLY. Well, hello, Andy.

AMOS. Amos. My name is Amos.

BILLY. Right. Did you bring the rest of the five thousand dollars?

AMOS. Well – here's five hundred on my insurance. And three hundred dollars that I borrowed from the guys at the garage. And seven hundred out of the building and loan fund –

BILLY. That's two thousand.

AMOS. And that's all I got so far.

BILLY. What about her father?

AMOS. I phoned him yesterday and he told me he'll probably be able to raise some money later.

BILLY. You're a damned liar. I spoke to her father myself. You know what he told me? That his daughter went to Hell ten years ago and she could stay there forever before he'd spend a cent to get her out.

AMOS. I'll pay you twenty dollars a week on my salary. I'll give you notes with interest – double, triple – till every cent is paid.

BILLY. You know, that's touching. But I've got a motto, and that motto is this – play square. Dead square. Now, when you came to me yesterday, I didn't ask you was she guilty. I didn't ask was she innocent. I didn't ask you if she was a drunk or a dope fiend. No foolish questions like that, now did I? No. All I said was, "Have you got five thousand dollars?" And you said yes. But you haven't got five thousand dollars so I figure you're a dirty liar.

AMOS. *(starts to take money, certificates, etc., back)* I'm sorry, Mr. Flynn.

BILLY. *(puts hand on money and takes it from **AMOS**)* But I took her case and I'll keep it because I play square.

BILLY. *(cont.)* Now look, Hart, I don't like to blow my own horn, but believe me, if Jesus Christ had lived in Chicago today – and if he had five thousand dollars – things would have turned out differently. Now, here's what we're gonna do. By tomorrow morning I'll have her name on every front page as the hottest little jazz slayer since Velma Kelly. Then we announce we're gonna hold an auction. To raise money for her defense. They'll buy anything she ever touched – shoes, dresses, underwear. Plus, we tell 'em that if by due process of law she gets hanged –

AMOS. Hanged?

BILLY. – the stuff triples in value. I'll give you twenty percent of everything we make over $5,000. And that's what I call playing square.

AMOS. I don't know, Mr. Flynn.

BILLY. You see, it's like this: either I get the entire five thousand –

([MUSIC: No. 8 – "$5,000 CUE"] as **AMOS** *exits.* **ROXIE** *enters.)*

(To **ROXIE***:)* – or you'll rot in jail before I bring you to trial.

ROXIE. Look, Mr. Flynn. I've never been very good at this sort of thing. But couldn't we possibly make some sort of arrangement between us?

BILLY. Hey, you mean one thing to me – five thousand bucks – and that's all. Get it? Now look, in a few minutes we're gonna have a big press conference here. There'll be a whole bunch of photographers and reporters and that sob sister from *The Evening Star* is coming.

[SONG: No. 9 – "A LITTLE BIT OF GOOD"]

(offstage coloratura trill)

I don't figure we'll have any trouble with her.

(another trill)

She'll swallow, hook, line, and sinker.

(another trill)

BILLY. *(cont.)*

Her name's Mary Sunshine.

*(**MARY SUNSHINE** enters.)*

MARY SUNSHINE.

WHEN I WAS A TINY TOT
OF MAYBE TWO OR THREE,
I CAN STILL REMEMBER
WHAT MY MOTHER SAID TO ME,
PLACE ROSE COLORED GLASSES ON YOUR NOSE
AND YOU WILL SEE THE ROBINS
NOT THE CROWS.

FOR IN THE TENSE AND TANGLED WEB
OUR WEARY LIVES CAN WEAVE,
YOU'RE SO MUCH BETTER OFF IF YOU
BELIEVE

THAT THERE'S A LITTLE BIT OF GOOD
IN EVERYONE.
IN EVERYONE YOU'LL EVER KNOW.

YES, THERE'S A LITTLE BIT OF GOOD
IN EVERYONE,
THOUGH MANY TIMES, IT DOESN'T SHOW.

IT ONLY TAKES THE TAKING TIME WITH ONE ANOTHER
FOR UNDER EVERY MEAN VENEER
IS SOMEONE WARM AND DEAR.
KEEP LOOKING

FOR THAT BIT OF GOOD IN EVERYONE
THE ONES WE CALL BAD
ARE NEVER ALL BAD.
SO TRY TO FIND THAT LITTLE BIT OF GOOD.

JUST A LITTLE LITTLE BIT OF GOOD.
HAH HAH HAH HAH.
AHHH

MARY SUNSHINE. (*cont.*)

> THERE'S SOMEONE WARM AND DEAR.
> KEEP LOOKING
> FOR THAT BIT OF GOOD IN EVERYONE.
>
> ALTHOUGH YOU MEET RATS,
> THEY'RE NOT COMPLETE RATS.
> SO TRY TO FIND THAT LITTLE BIT OF GOOD.

*(**MARY SUNSHINE** exits.)*

ROXIE. Mary Sunshine is going to interview me! Holy crap!

BILLY. Hey, and pipe down on the swearin'. From here on in, you say nothin' rougher than, "Oh, dear." Get it? Now the first thing we got to do is go after sympathy from the Press. They're not all pushovers like that Mary Sunshine. Chicago is a tough town. It's gotten so tough that they shoot the girls right out from under you. But there's one thing that they can never resist and that's a reformed sinner – so I've decided to rewrite the story of your life. "From Convent to Jail." Get this.

[MUSIC: No. 10 – "ROXIE'S STORY"]

Beautiful Southern home. Every luxury and refinement. Parents dead, educated at the Sacred Heart, fortune swept away – a run away marriage, a lovely, innocent girl, bewildered by what's happened –young, full of life, lonely, you where caught up by the mad whirl of a great city –

[MUSIC: Underscoring changes]

– jazz, cabarets, liquor –

*(**ROXIE** getting caught up, rises)*

Sit down. You were drawn like a moth to the flame. And now, the mad whirl has ceased. A butterfly crushed on the wheel.

[MUSIC out]

You have sinned and you are sorry.

ROXIE. God, that's beautiful.

BILLY. And cut out God, too. Stay where you're better acquainted. Now, when they ask you why you killed him – all you can remember is a fearful quarrel and he threatened to kill you. You can still see him coming toward you with that awful look in his eyes. And get this – you both reached for the gun.

[MUSIC: Rim shot]

That's your grounds. Self-defense.

[SONG: No. 11 – "WE BOTH REACH FOR THE GUN"]

(**MATRON** *enters.*)

MATRON. Mr. Flynn, the reporters are here.

BILLY. Let 'em in, Butch.

([MUSIC: Drum roll] **ENSEMBLE** *and* **MARY SUNSHINE** *enter.*)

BILLY. Well good day, Ladies and Gentlemen. Miss Sunshine. You know my client, Miss Roxie Hart.

ROXIE. Ladies and Gentlemen, I'm just so flattered y'all came to see l'il ol' me. I guess you want to know why I shot the bastard.

BILLY. Sit down, dummy.

(**BILLY** *grabs* **ROXIE** *and sits her on his knee like a ventriloquist's dummy.*)

MATRON. Mr. Billy Flynn sings the "Press Conference Rag" – notice how his mouth never moves – almost.

ENSEMBLE.
WHERE'D YOU COME FROM?

BILLY. *(as* **ROXIE***)*
MISSISSIPPI.

ENSEMBLE.
AND YOUR PARENTS?

BILLY. *(as* **ROXIE***)*
VERY WEALTHY.

ENSEMBLE.
WHERE ARE THEY NOW?

BILLY. *(as* **ROXIE***)*

   SIX FEET UNDER.

BILLY.

   BUT SHE WAS GRANTED ONE MORE START,

BILLY. *(as* **ROXIE***)*

   THE CONVENT OF THE SACRED HEART.

ENSEMBLE.

   WHEN'D YOU GET HERE?

BILLY. *(as* **ROXIE***)*

   1920.

ENSEMBLE.

   HOW OLD WERE YOU?

BILLY. *(as* **ROXIE***)*

   DON'T REMEMBER.

ENSEMBLE.

   THEN WHAT HAPPENED?

BILLY. *(as* **ROXIE***)*

   I MET AMOS.

   AND HE STOLE MY HEART AWAY,

   CONVINCED ME TO ELOPE ONE DAY.

MARY SUNSHINE. A convent girl! A run away marriage! Oh,
   it's too terrible. You poor, poor dear.

ENSEMBLE.

   WHO'S FRED CASELY?

BILLY. *(as* **ROXIE***)*

   MY EX-BOY FRIEND.

ENSEMBLE.

   WHY'D YOU SHOOT HIM?

BILLY. *(as* **ROXIE***)*

   I WAS LEAVIN'.

ENSEMBLE.

   WAS HE ANGRY?

BILLY. *(as* **ROXIE***)*

   LIKE A MADMAN!

   STILL I SAID, "FRED, MOVE ALONG."

BILLY. *(spoken)* She knew that she was doin' wrong.

ENSEMBLE.

    THEN DESCRIBE IT.

BILLY. *(as* **ROXIE***)*

    HE CAME TOWARD ME.

ENSEMBLE.

    WITH THE PISTOL?

BILLY. *(as* **ROXIE***)*

    FROM MY BUREAU.

ENSEMBLE.

    DID YOU FIGHT HIM?

BILLY. *(as* **ROXIE***)*

    LIKE A TIGER.

BILLY. *(spoken)* He had strength and she had none –

BILLY. *(as* **ROXIE***)*

    AND YET WE BOTH REACHED FOR THE GUN.

    OH YES, OH YES, OH YES, WE BOTH,

    OH YES, WE BOTH,

    OH YES, WE BOTH REACHED FOR

    THE GUN, THE GUN, THE GUN, THE GUN,

    OH YES, WE BOTH REACHED FOR THE GUN,

    FOR THE GUN.

BILLY & ENSEMBLE.

    OH YES, OH YES, OH YES, THEY BOTH,

    OH YES, THEY BOTH,

    OH YES, THEY BOTH REACHED FOR

    THE GUN, THE GUN, THE GUN, THE GUN,

    OH YES, THEY BOTH REACHED FOR THE GUN,

    FOR THE GUN.

BILLY.

    UNDERSTANDABLE, UNDERSTANDABLE.

    YES, IT'S PERFECTLY UNDERSTANDABLE.

    COMPREHENSIBLE, COMPREHENSIBLE.

    NOT A BIT REPREHENSIBLE,

    IT'S SO DEFENSIBLE.

ENSEMBLE.

    HOW'RE YOU FEELING?

BILLY. *(as* **ROXIE***)*
>   VERY FRIGHTENED.

ENSEMBLE.
>   ARE YOU SORRY?

BILLY. *(as herself)*
>   ARE YOU KIDDING?

ENSEMBLE.
>   WHAT'S YOUR STATEMENT?

BILLY. *(as* **ROXIE***)*
>   ALL I'D SAY IS
>   THOUGH MY CHOO-CHOO JUMPED THE TRACK,
>   I'D GIVE MY LIFE TO BRING HIM BACK.

ENSEMBLE.
>   AND?

BILLY. *(as* **ROXIE***)*
>   STAY AWAY FROM

ENSEMBLE.
>   WHAT?

BILLY. *(as* **ROXIE***)*
>   JAZZ AND LIQUOR

ENSEMBLE.
>   AND?

BILLY. *(as* **ROXIE***)*
>   AND THE MEN WHO

ENSEMBLE.
>   WHAT?

BILLY. *(as* **ROXIE***)*
>   PLAY FOR FUN!

ENSEMBLE.
>   AND WHAT?

BILLY. *(as* **ROXIE***)*
>   THAT'S THE THOUGHT THAT

ENSEMBLE.
>   YEAH?

BILLY. *(as* **ROXIE***)*
>   CAME UPON ME

ENSEMBLE.

WHEN?

BILLY. *(as* **ROXIE***)*

WHEN WE BOTH REACHED FOR THE GUN.

MARY SUNSHINE.

UNDERSTANDABLE, UNDERSTANDABLE.

BILLY & MARY SUNSHINE.

YES, IT'S PERFECTLY UNDERSTANDABLE.
COMPREHENSIBLE, COMPREHENSIBLE.
NOT A BIT REPREHENSIBLE,
IT'S SO DEFENSIBLE.

BILLY.	**ENSEMBLE.**
	OH YES, OH YES, OH YES,
Let me hear it!	THEY BOTH,
	OH YES, THEY BOTH,
A little louder!	OH YES, THEY BOTH REACHED FOR THE GUN, THE GUN, THE GUN THE GUN,
	OH YES, THE BOTH REACHED FOR THE GUN, FOR THE GUN.
	OH YES, OH YES, OH YES,
	THEY BOTH,
	OH YES, THEY BOTH,
Now you got it!	OH YES, THEY BOTH REACHED FOR THE GUN, THE GUN, THE GUN THE GUN,
	OH YES, THEY BOTH REACHED FOR THE GUN, FOR THE GUN.

MARY SUNSHINE/ENSEMBLE.

OH YES, OH YES, OH YES, THEY BOTH,
OH YES, THEY BOTH,
OH YES, THEY BOTH REACHED FOR
THE GUN, THE GUN, THE GUN, THE GUN,
OH YES, THEY BOTH REACHED FOR THE GUN,
FOR THE GUN.

MARY SUNSHINE/ENSEMBLE. (*cont.*)

OH YES, OH YES, OH YES, THEY BOTH,
OH YES, THEY BOTH,
OH YES, THEY BOTH REACHED FOR
THE GUN, THE GUN, THE GUN, THE GUN,
THE GUN, THE GUN, THE GUN, THE GUN,
THE GUN, THE GUN, THE GUN, THE GUN,
THE GUN, THE GUN, THE GUN, THE GUN,

BILLY.

BOTH REACHED FOR THE GUN.

MARY SUNSHINE/ENSEMBLE.

THE GUN, THE GUN, THE GUN, THE GUN,
THE GUN, THE GUN, THE GUN, THE GUN,
THE GUN, THE GUN, THE GUN, THE GUN,
THE GUN, THE GUN, THE GUN, THE GUN,
BOTH REACHED FOR THE GUN!

Scene Nine

[MUSIC: No. 12 – "1ST NEWSPAPER HEADLINES"]

ENSEMBLE MEMBER #7. Stop the presses!

ENSEMBLE MEMBER #6. "Convent Girl Held!"

ENSEMBLE MEMBER #8. "'We Both Reached for the Gun,' says Roxie!"

ENSEMBLE MEMBER #2. "'Dancing Feet Lead to Sorrow' says Beautiful Jazz Slayer!"

MARY SUNSHINE. "Roxie sobs, 'I'd Give Anything to Bring Him Back!'"

ENSEMBLE MEMBER #5. "'Jazz and Liquor Roxie's Downfall!'" *(Underscoring stops.)* Ya got that, Charlie? Right.

([SONG: No. 13 – "ROXIE"] as **ENSEMBLE** *exits.)*

ROXIE. You wanna know something? I always wanted my name in the paper. Before Amos, I used to date this well-to-do, ugly bootlegger. He used to like to dress me up, take me out and show me off. Ugly guys like to do that. Once it said in the paper, "Gangland's Al Capelli seen at Chez Vito with cute redheaded chorine." That was me. I clipped it out and saved it. Now look, "ROXIE ROCKS CHICAGO." Look, I'm gonna tell you the truth. Not that the truth really matters, but I'm gonna tell you anyway. The thing is, see I'm older than I ever intended to be. All my life I wanted to be a dancer in vaudeville. Oh, yeah. Have my own act. But, no. No. No. No. No. No. It was one big world full of "No." Life. Then Amos came along. Sweet, safe Amos, who never says no. You know some guys are like mirrors, and when I catch myself in Amos' face I'm always a kid. Ya could love a guy like that. Look now, I gotta tell ya, and I hope this ain't too crude. In the bed department, Amos was…zero. I mean, when we went to bed, he made love to me like he was fixin' a carburetor or somethin'. "I love ya, honey. I love ya." Anyway, to make a long story short, I started foolin' around.

ROXIE. *(cont.)* Then I started screwin' around, which is foolin' around without dinner. I gave up the vaudeville idea, because after all those years....well, you sort of figure opportunity just passed you by. Oh, but it ain't. Oh no, no, no, but it ain't. If this Flynn guy gets me off, and with all this publicity, I could still get into vaudeville. I could still have my own act. Now, I got me a world full of "Yes."

THE NAME ON EVERYBODY'S LIPS
IS GONNA BE ROXIE.
THE LADY RAKIN' IN THE CHIPS
IS GONNA BE ROXIE.

I'M GONNA BE A CELEBRITY.
THAT MEANS SOMEBODY EVERYONE KNOWS.
THEY'RE GONNA RECOGNIZE MY EYES,
MY HAIR, MY TEETH, MY BOOBS, MY NOSE.

FROM JUST SOME DUMB MECHANIC'S WIFE,
I'M GONNA BE ROXIE.
WHO SAYS THAT MURDER'S NOT AN ART?

AND WHO IN CASE SHE DOESN'T HANG
CAN SAY SHE STARTED WITH A BANG?
ROXIE HART!

I'm going to have a swell act, too! Yeah, I'll get a boy to work with – someone who can lift me up and show me off – Oh, Hell, I'll get two boys. It'll frame me better! Think big, Roxie, think big – I'm gonna get me a whole bunch of boys.

*(**ENSEMBLE MEN** enter.)*

THE NAME ON EVERYBODY'S LIPS
IS GONNA BE

ENSEMBLE MEN. *(whispered)* Roxie!

ROXIE.

THE LADY RAKIN' IN THE CHIPS
IS GONNA BE

ENSEMBLE MEN. *(whispered)* Roxie!

SHE'S GONNA BE A CELEBRITY.

ROXIE.

THAT MEANS SOMEBODY EVERYONE KNOWS.

ENSEMBLE MEN. Yeah!

THEY'RE GONNA RECOGNIZE HER EYES,
HER HAIR, HER TEETH,

ROXIE.

MY BOOBS, MY NOSE.
FROM JUST SOME DUMB MECHANIC'S WIFE,
I'M GONNA BE

Sing it!

ENSEMBLE MEN.

ROXIE!

ROXIE.

WHO SAYS THAT MURDER'S NOT AN ART?

ENSEMBLE MEN.

AND WHO IN CASE SHE DOESN'T HANG

ROXIE.

CAN SAY SHE STARTED WITH A BANG?
FOXY

ROXIE/ENSEMBLE MEN.

ROXIE HART!

ENSEMBLE MEN.

CHUH,
CHUH. CHUH. CHUH, CHUH. CHUH,
CHUH, CHUH,
CHUH, CHUH, CHUH, CHUH, CHUH,
CHUH, CHUH
CHUH, CHUH, CHUH, CHUH, CHUH

THEY'RE GONNA WAIT OUTSIDE IN LINE
TO GET TO SEE ROXIE.

ROXIE.

THINK OF THOSE AUTOGRAPHS I'LL SIGN
"GOOD LUCK TO YOU, ROXIE!"
AND I'LL APPEAR IN A LAVALIERE
THAT GOES ALL THE WAY DOWN TO MY WAIST.

ENSEMBLE MEN.

    HERE A RING, THERE A RING.

    EVERYWHERE A RING A LING.

ROXIE.

    BUT ALWAYS IN THE BEST OF TASTE.

    Ooo, I'm a star.

ENSEMBLE MEN. And the audience loves her.

ROXIE. And I love the audience. And the audience loves me for loving them. And I love the audience for loving me. And we just love each other. And that's because none of us got enough love in our childhood.

ENSEMBLE MEN. That's right.

ROXIE. And that's show biz, kid.

ENSEMBLE MEN. Oh, yeah.

    SHE'S GIVING UP HER HUMDRUM LIFE.

ROXIE.

    I'M GONNA BE –

ENSEMBLE MEN.

    ROXIE

    (whispered) She made a scandal

    (sung)

    AND A START.

ROXIE.

    AND SOPHIE TUCKER'LL SHIT, I KNOW,

ENSEMBLE MEN. Uh-huh!

ROXIE.

    TO SEE HER NAME GET BILLED BELOW

ALL.

    FOXY ROXIE HART.

ENSEMBLE MEN. *(ad-lib)*

    CHUH, CHUH, CHUH, ETC...

ROXIE. *(as ENSEMBLE MEN exit)* Those are my boys.

    (ROXIE exits.)

Scene Ten

(The jail.)

[MUSIC: No. 14 – "2ND NEWSPAPER HEADLINES"]

ENSEMBLE MEMBER #8. "Roxie Rocks Chicago!"

ENSEMBLE MEMBER #3. "Fans Riot at Roxie Auction!"

MATRON. *(entering)* "Roxie's Nightie Raises 200 Bucks!"

VELMA. Mama, you know that I am not a jealous person, but every time I see that tomato's name on the front-page – it drives me nertz.

MATRON. Baby, I got some bad news.

VELMA. What do you mean?

MATRON. I mean, the tour. It's canceled.

VELMA. Canceled!

MATRON. Well, your name hasn't been in the papers for a long time. I been getting calls from the boys at William Morris all day. "We've lost interest." "We don't want her." "She's washed up." "She's a bum." Do you know how it hurts Mama to hear that about someone she cares for?

VELMA. Oh, sure.

MATRON. All you read about today is the Hart kid.

VELMA. Hey, Mama, I've got an idea.

[SONG: No. 15 – "I CAN'T DO IT ALONE"]

Suppose I talk Hart into doing that sister act with me?

MATRON. Ladies and Gentlemen, Miss Velma Kelly in an act of desperation.

(VELMA approaches ROXIE.)

VELMA.

MY SISTER AND I HAD AN ACT THAT COULDN'T FLOP.
MY SISTER AND I WERE HEADED STRAIGHT FOR THE TOP.
MY SISTER AND I EARNED A THOU A WEEK AT LEAST.

Oh yeah.

BUT MY SISTER IS NOW, UNFORTUNATELY, DECEASED.

VELMA. *(cont.)* I know,

IT'S SAD, OF COURSE, BUT A FACT
IS STILL A FACT.
AND NOW ALL THAT REMAINS
IS THE REMAINS OF A PERFECT DOUBLE ACT

Do you know that you are exactly the same size as my sister? You would fit in her wardrobe perfectly. Look, why don't I show you some of the act, huh? Watch this.

(dance)

Now, you have to imagine it with two people. It's swell with two people.

FIRST I'D...

*(**VELMA** imitates drums.)*

Drums!

THEN SHE'D...

*(**VELMA** imitates saxophone.)*

Saxophone!

THEN WE'D...

*(**VELMA** ad libs together.)*

Together!

BUT I CAN'T DO IT ALONE.

THEN SHE'D...
THEN I'D...
THEN WE'D...
BUT I CAN'T DO IT ALONE.

SHE'D SAY, "WHAT'S YOUR SISTER LIKE?"
I'D SAY, "MEN." YUK, YUK, YUK.

SHE'D SAY, "YOU'RE THE CAT'S MEOW"
THEN WE'D WOW THE CROWD AGAIN WHEN

SHE'D GO...
I'D GO...
WE'D GO...

VELMA. *(cont.)*

THEN THOSE DING DONG DADDIES STARTED TO ROAR
WHISTLED, STOMPED AND STAMPED ON THE FLOOR
YELLING, SCREAMING, BEGGING FOR MORE.

And we'd say, "O.K. fellas, keep your socks up. You ain't seen nothin' yet!"

(dance)

BUT I SIMPLY CANNOT DO IT ALONE.

Well? What did ya think? Come on, you can say.

(**ROXIE** *gives her a raspberry.*)

O.K., O.K. The first part can always be rewritten. But the second part was really nifty. Watch this.

THEN SHE'D...
THEN I'D...
THEN WE'D...
BUT I CAN'T DO IT ALONE.

SHE'D SAY, "WHAT STATE'S CHICAGO IN?"
I'D SAY, "ILL."

Ya get that?

SHE'D SAY, "TURN YOUR MOTOR OFF."

(dance)

I CAN HEAR 'EM CHEERIN' STILL WHEN

SHE'D GO...
I'D GO...
WE'D GO...

AND THEN THOSE TWO-BIT JOHNNIES DID IT UP BROWN
TO CHEER THE BEST ATTRACTION IN TOWN.
THEY NEARLY TORE THE BALCONY DOWN.

And we'd say, "O.K. boys, we're goin' home, but here's a few more partin' shots!." And this....this we did in perfect unison.

(dance)

VELMA. *(cont.)*

NOW, YOU'VE SEEN ME GOIN' THROUGH IT,
IT MAY SEEM THERE'S NOTHIN' TO IT.
BUT I SIMPLY CANNOT DO IT ALONE!

Ah, well…?

ROXIE. Boy, they sure got lousy floorshows in jails now-a-days. I mean, there was a time when you could go to jail and get a really….

VELMA. O.K. Roxie! I'll level with ya.

ROXIE. Listen, what did Mama just tell ya? It's me they want now, huh? Haven't you read the papers lately? I'm a star – I'm a big star *single*.

VELMA. Thanks.

ROXIE. Nothin' personal, you understand.

(**ROXIE** *exits.*)

VELMA. Nothin' personal. Nothin's ever personal.

[SONG: No. 16 – "I CAN'T DO IT ALONE – TAG"]

LIKE THE DESERTED BRIDE ON HER WEDDING NIGHT,
ALL ALONE AND SHAKING WITH FRIGHT,
WITH HER BRAND NEW HUBBY NOWHERE IN SIGHT,
I SIMPLY CANNOT DO IT ALONE.

(**VELMA** *exits.*)

[MUSIC: No. 17 – "CHICAGO AFTER MIDNIGHT"]

MATRON. Well, here's the way I got the story. There's this Kitty-something or other. I didn't catch her last name.

(**GO-TO-HELL KITTY** *enters.*)

Anyway, she's some sort of heiress. Her folks are in pineapples, grapefruits, somethin' like that. Well, she's playing house in a Northside apartment with a guy named Harry. Harry spends all his time in bed. You know, a real mattress dancer. Last night this Kitty dame comes home. Harry's already in bed. She goes to change. And when she returns, she notices something rather odd.

(**KITTY** *sees* **HARRY** *with* **ENSEMBLE MEMBER #9**.)

MATRON. *(cont.)* Very odd.

(**KITTY** *sees* **ENSEMBLE MEMBER #10** *with* **HARRY** *as well.*)

Extremely odd.

(**KITTY** *sees* **ENSEMBLE MEMBER #6** *with* **HARRY** *and the women.*)

Puzzled. She disappears for a second. When she returns she gently awakens Harry.

[MUSIC out]

KITTY. Oh, Harry…

HARRY. O.K. Are you gonna believe what you see or what I tell you?

KITTY. What I see!

[MUSIC: No. 18 – "3RD NEWSPAPER HEADLINE"]

(**KITTY** *shoots* **HARRY** *and the three* **ENSEMBLE MEMBERS** *– two times – with machine gun blasts.*)

ENSEMBLE MEMBER #2. "Lake Shore Drive Massacre!"

ENSEMBLE MEMBER #11. "Berserk Filly Fells Four!"

MARY SUNSHINE. "Gang in Bed – All Dead!"

Scene Eleven

(The jail.)

BILLY. Gentlemen, please, my client will be happy to answer all your questions!

(KITTY bites BILLY.)

Ow, will you stop biting? I'll get hydrophobia.

KITTY. Go to hell. Go to hell all of you. I'm not answering any more questions.

MATRON. Come on, Dearie. I'm gonna show you to your suite. You're gonna love it.

KITTY. Wait a minute! Do you know who my father is?

ENSEMBLE. Who?

KITTY. Well, he owns all of Hawaii! So go to hell! You GO TO HELL!

(KITTY and the REPORTERS start to exit.)

BILLY. Step right in here, Gentlemen. She will answer all your questions and afterwards I'll be happy to give you an interview myself...

ROXIE. Mr. Flynn! Mr. Flynn!

BILLY. Hi, Trixie.

ROXIE. Trixie?

BILLY. Oh, I mean Roxie. Boy, what a hellion, huh? And a socialite, too! Her mother owns all the pineapples in Hawaii.

ROXIE. What the hell do I care about pineapples? Did ya get my trial date?

BILLY. Take it easy, kid. I'll get to it.

VELMA. Mr. Flynn. There's a couple of things I'd like to discuss about my trial, too.

BILLY. Oh yeah...Hi ya, Velma. First things first, honey.

(to MARY) Oh Miss Sunshine? Can I call you "Mary"? The girl's from old pineapple money. It's a gripping story really...

(**MARY** *and* **BILLY** *exit.*)

ROXIE. Pineapples. I got a feeling you're in trouble, Roxie.

VELMA. Socialite. You lose again, Velma.

ROXIE. There's only one person who can help you now, Roxie.

VELMA. There's only one person you can count on now, Velma.

CONDUCTOR. And now, Miss Roxie Hart and Miss Velma Kelly sing a song of unrelenting determination and unmitigated ego.

[SONG: No. 19 – "MY OWN BEST FRIEND"]

ROXIE.

ONE THING I KNOW

VELMA.

ONE THING I KNOW

ROXIE.

AND I'VE ALWAYS KNOWN,

VELMA.

AND I'VE ALWAYS KNOWN,

ROXIE.

I AM MY OWN

VELMA.

I AM MY OWN

VELMA/ROXIE.

BEST FRIEND.

ROXIE.

BABY'S ALIVE

VELMA.

BABY'S ALIVE

ROXIE.

BUT BABY'S ALONE,

VELMA.

BUT BABY'S ALONE,

ROXIE.

AND BABY'S HER OWN

VELMA.

AND BABY'S HER OWN

VELMA/ROXIE.

BEST FRIEND.
MANY'S THE GUY
WHO TOLD ME HE CARES,
BUT THEY WERE SCRATCHIN' MY BACK
'CAUSE I WAS SCRATCHIN' THEIRS.

ROXIE.

AND TRUSTING TO LUCK,
(**ROXIE** *laughs.*)

VELMA.

AND TRUSTING TO LUCK,
(**VELMA** *laughs.*)

ROXIE.

THAT'S ONLY FOR FOOLS,

VELMA.

THAT'S ONLY FOR FOOLS,

ROXIE.

I PLAY IN A GAME

VELMA.

I PLAY IN A GAME

VELMA/ROXIE.

WHERE I MAKE THE RULES.

VELMA.

WHERE I MAKE THE RULES.
AND RULE NUMBER ONE
FROM HERE TO THE END
IS I AM MY OWN BEST FRIEND.

VELMA/ROXIE.	**ENSEMBLE.**
THREE MUSKETEERS	AH
WHO NEVER SAY DIE	AH
ARE STANDING HERE	
THIS MINUTE	

VELMA.

ME,

ROXIE.

ME,

VELMA.

MYSELF,

ROXIE.

MYSELF,

VELMA.

AND I.

ROXIE.

AND I.

ENSEMBLE.

AND I

AND I

AND I

I, I, I

ROXIE/VELMA.	**ENSEMBLE.**
IF LIFE IS A SCHOOL,	AH
I'LL PASS EVERY TEST.	AH
IF LIFE IS A GAME,	AH
I'LL PLAY IT THE BEST.	AH
'CAUSE I WON'T GIVE IN,	
AND I'LL NEVER BEND,	
AND I AM MY OWN BEST FRIEND.	

*(***ROXIE*** faints.)*

VELMA. What the hell was that?

ROXIE.. Mr. Flynn? Miss Sunshine? And all you reporters!

*(***ROXIE*** faints again.)*

Oh, don't worry about me. It's just that I'm going to have a baby.

ENSEMBLE. A baby!

[MUSIC: No. 20 – "FIRST ACT CURTAIN"]

VELMA. Shit.

BILLY. I want the best doctor in the city for my poor client. Somebody pick that girl up.

VELMA.

AND ALL THAT JAZZ!

(Curtain)

ACT TWO

[MUSIC: No. 21 – "ENTR' ACTE"]

Scene 1

(The jail.)

VELMA. Hello suckers, welcome back. Roxie's in there being looked over by the State Medical Examiner. She says she's gonna have a baby. Now why didn't I think of that?

[SONG: No. 22 – "I KNOW A GIRL"]

CAN YOU IMAGINE?
I MEAN CAN YOU IMAGINE?

CAN YOU BELIEVE IT?
I MEAN, CAN YOU BELIEVE IT?

I KNOW A GIRL,
A GIRL WHO LANDS ON TOP.
YOU COULD PUT HER FACE INTO A PAIL OF SLOP
AND SHE'D COME UP SMELLING LIKE A ROSE.
HOW SHE DOES IT, HEAVEN KNOWS.

SECOND REPORTER. Hold on everybody, she's comin' out now.

(ROXIE and a DOCTOR enter.)

Well, Doc, is she or isn't she?

VELMA. She is.

SECOND REPORTER. She is.

VELMA.

I KNOW A GIRL,
A GIRL WITH SO MUCH LUCK.
SHE COULD GET RUN OVER BY A TWO-TON TRUCK
THEN BRUSH HERSELF OFF AND WALK AWAY.
HOW SHE DOES IT, COULDN'T SAY.

BILLY. Doc, would you swear to that statement in court?

DOCTOR. Yes.

BILLY. Good. Uh…button your fly.

*(**BILLY** and the **DOCTOR** exit.)*

VELMA.

WHILST I,
ON THE OTHER HAND,
PUT MY FACE IN A PAIL OF SLOP
AND I WOULD SMELL LIKE A PAIL OF SLOP.
I, ON THE OTHER HAND,
GET RUN OVER BY A TRUCK
AND I AM DEADER THAN A DUCK.

I KNOW A GIRL
WHO TELLS SO MANY LIES,
ANYTHING THAT'S TRUE WOULD TRULY CROSS HER EYES.
BUT WHAT THAT MOUSE IS SELLING,
THE WHOLE WORLD BUYS
AND NOBODY SMELLS A RAT.

ROXIE. Please, Ladies and Gentlemen of the press – leave the two of us alone so we can rest.

VELMA. The two of us?

CAN YOU IMAGINE?
I MEAN, CAN YOU IMAGINE?

THIRD REPORTER. Could I have one last picture please?

ROXIE. Sure, anything for the press.

VELMA.

DO YOU BELIEVE IT?
I MEAN, DO YOU BELIEVE IT?

[SONG: No. 23 – "ME AND MY BABY"]

ROXIE.

MY DEAR LITTLE BABY,

VELMA. *(imitating **ROXIE**)*

MY DEAR LITTLE BABY,

ROXIE.

MY SWEET LITTLE BABY,

VELMA. *(imitating* **ROXIE***)*

MY SWEET LITTLE BABY.

ROXIE.

LOOK AT MY BABY AND ME.
ME AND MY BABY,
MY BABY AND ME,
WE'RE 'BOUT AS HAPPY AS BABIES CAN BE.
WHAT IF I FIND
THAT I'M CAUGHT IN A STORM?
I DON'T CARE,
MY BABY'S THERE,
AND BABY'S BOUND TO KEEP ME WARM.

WE'RE STICKING TOGETHER
AND AIN'T WE GOT FUN?
SO MUCH TOGETHER
YOU'D COUNT US AS ONE.
TELL OLD MAN WORRY TO GO CLIMB A TREE,
'CAUSE I'VE GOT MY BABY,
MY SWEET LITTLE BABY,
LOOK AT MY BABY AND ME.

MARY SUNSHINE. I don't see how you could possibly delay the trial another second, Mr. Flynn. My readers wouldn't stand for it. The poor child! To have her baby born in a jail!

BILLY FLYNN. I can assure you she'll come to trial at the earliest possible moment. And you can quote me on that.

AMOS. Hey, everybody. I'm the father! I'm the father!

ROXIE & ENSEMBLE MEN. *(spoken)* Yuck, yuck, yuck, yuck.

ROXIE.

LOOK AT MY BABY,
MY BABY AND ME.
A DREAM OF A DUO,
NOW DON'T YOU AGREE?
WHY KEEP IT MUM
WHEN THERE'S NOTHING TO HIDE?
AND WHAT I FEEL,
I MUST REVEAL
IT'S MORE THAN I CAN KEEP INSIDE.

ROXIE. *(cont.)*

> I CAN ASSURE YOU
> IT WON'T GO AWAY.
> LET ME ASSURE YOU
> IT GROWS EVERY DAY.
>
> I WAS A "ONE" ONCE
> BUT NOW I'M A "WE",
> 'CAUSE I GOT MY BABY,
> MY SWEET LITTLE BABY,
> MY DEAR LITTLE BABY,
> LOOK AT MY BABY AND ME.

MATRON. I think it's sweet. First time we ever had one of our girls knocked up.

BILLY. I've got it and it's brilliant. I'm gonna get Amos to divorce you. That way all the sympathy will go to you – not him. You'll be the poor, little deserted mother-to-be and that crumb is running out on you.

AMOS. That's my kid! That's my kid!

ROXIE & ENSEMBLE MEN/WOMEN.

> LOOK-A MY BABY,
> MY BABY AND ME
> FACING THE WORLD
> OPTIMISTICALLY.
> NOTHING CAN STOP US,
> SO NOBODY TRY,
> 'CAUSE BABY'S ROUGH
> AND FULL OF STUFF
> AND INCIDENTALLY, SO AM I.
>
> *(dance to:)*

ROXIE & ENSEMBLE MEN.

> MAMA, MAMA,
> MAMA, MAMA,
> MAMA, MAMA,
> MAMA!

ENSEMBLE MEN/ENSEMBLE WOMEN.

GET OUT OF OUR WAY, FOLKS,
AND GIVE US SOME ROOM.
WATCH HOW WE BUBBLE
AND BLOSSOM AND BLOOM.
LIFE WAS A PRISON
BUT WE GOT THE KEY,
ME AND MY BABY,
MY DEAR LITTLE BABY,
MY CUTE LITTLE BABY,
MY SWEET LITTLE BABY,
MY FAT LITTLE BABY,
MY SOFT LITTLE BABY,
MY PINK LITTLE BABY,
MY BALD LITTLE BABY,
LOOK-A MY BABY

ROXIE.

AND ME.

(**ROXIE** and **ENSEMBLE MEN** exit.)

[SONG: No. 24 – "MISTER CELLOPHANE"]

AMOS. I'm the father! Papa! Dada! Did you hear me? Did you? No, you didn't hear me. That's the story of my life. Nobody ever listens to me. Have you noticed that? Am I making it up? Nobody ever knows I'm around. Nobody. Ever. Not even my parents noticed me. One day I went to school and when I came home...

[MUSIC out]

...they'd moved.

[MUSIC in]

IF SOMEONE STOOD UP IN A CROWD,
AND RAISED HIS VOICE UP WAY OUT LOUD,
AND WAVED HIS ARM,
AND SHOOK HIS LEG...
YOU'D NOTICE HIM.

AMOS. *(cont.)*

> IF SOMEONE IN THE MOVIE SHOW
> YELLED, "FIRE IN THE SECOND ROW!
> THIS WHOLE PLACE IS A POWDER KEG!"
> YOU'D NOTICE HIM.
>
> AND EVEN WITHOUT CLUCKING LIKE A HEN,
> EVERYONE GETS NOTICED, NOW AND THEN,
> UNLESS, OF COURSE, THAT PERSONAGE SHOULD BE
> INVISIBLE, INCONSEQUENTIAL ME.
>
> CELLOPHANE,
> MISTER CELLOPHANE.
> SHOULD HAVE BEEN MY NAME,
>
> MISTER CELLOPHANE.
> 'CAUSE YOU CAN LOOK RIGHT THROUGH ME,
> WALK RIGHT BY ME
> AND NEVER KNOW I'M THERE.
>
> I TELL YA,
> CELLOPHANE,
> MISTER CELLOPHANE,
> SHOULD HAVE BEEN MY NAME,
> MISTER CELLOPHANE,
> 'CAUSE YOU CAN LOOK RIGHT THROUGH ME,
> WALK RIGHT BY ME,
> AND NEVER KNOW I'M THERE.

BILLY. Oh, Andy. I didn't see you there.

AMOS. Amos. My name is Amos.

BILLY. Who said it wasn't? It's the kid's name I'm thinkin' about.

AMOS. What kid?

BILLY. Roxie's kid. You know when she's due? Early Fall. September. Can you count? September. That means you couldn't possibly be...the father. But I want you to pass out those cigars anyway. I don't want you to give a damn when people...laugh.

AMOS. Laugh? Why would they laugh?

BILLY. Because they can count. Can you count? Early Fall? Here's a copy of Roxie's first statement. It says she hadn't copulated with you for four months prior to the...incident.

AMOS. That's right. We hadn't done no copulating for four months...early Fall. Now, wait a minute.

BILLY. But I want you to forget all that! My client needs your support.

AMOS. Well, that don't figure out right. I couldn't be the father.

BILLY. Divorce her? *[MUSIC out]* Is that what you said? My God man, you wouldn't divorce her! Over a little thing like that, would ya?

AMOS. You're damned right. That's what I'll do. I'll divorce her! She probably won't even notice.

BILLY. Are you still here, Andy? I thought you'd gone.

AMOS. Yeah, I'm still here. I think. *[MUSIC in]*

SUPPOSE YOU WAS A LITTLE CAT
RESIDIN' IN A PERSON'S FLAT,
WHO FED YOU FISH AND SCRATCHED YOUR EARS.
YOU'D NOTICE HIM.

SUPPOSE YOU WAS A WOMAN, WED
AND SLEEPIN' IN A DOUBLE BED,
BESIDE ONE MAN, FOR SEVEN YEARS.
YOU'D NOTICE HIM.

A HUMAN BEING'S MADE OF MORE THAN AIR.
WITH ALL THAT BULK, YOU'RE BOUND TO SEE HIM THERE.
UNLESS THAT HUMAN BEING NEXT TO YOU
IS UNIMPRESSIVE, UNDISTINGUISHED
YOU KNOW WHO.

SHOULD HAVE BEEN MY NAME,
MISTER CELLOPHANE,
'CAUSE YOU CAN LOOK RIGHT THROUGH ME,
WALK RIGHT BY ME,
AND NEVER KNOW I'M THERE.

AMOS. *(cont.)*

> I TELL YA,
> CELLOPHANE,
> MISTER CELLOPHANE,
> SHOULD HAVE BEEN MY NAME,
> MISTER CELLOPHANE,
>
> 'CAUSE YOU CAN LOOK RIGHT THROUGH ME,
> WALK RIGHT BY ME,
> AND NEVER KNOW I'M THERE.
> NEVER EVEN KNOW I'M THERE.

Hope I didn't take up too much of your time.

*(**AMOS** exits.)*

Scene Two

(The jail.)

BILLY. *(Entering. To the* **MATRON***)* Hello ladies! Hey, Diesel, get Roxie for me, will ya?

*(***MATRON*** exits.)*

VELMA. Billy, am I glad to see you. Look, March 5th is only a few weeks away and I've been makin' plans. Look.

*(***VELMA*** shows* **BILLY** *a pair of rhinestone buckles.)*

For the trial. Silver shoes with rhinestone buckles!

BILLY. Look, kid, your trial date's been set back.

VELMA. Oh, no!

BILLY. Less than a month. I had to, sweetie.

VELMA. And who got my date as if I didn't know, Roxie Hart?

BILLY. Hey, there's a lot of pressure on me. She's having a baby, f'chrissakes.

VELMA. Yeah, tell me about it. Listen Flynn, I figure if I am sensational in court I could get things moving again. I've been thinkin' a lot about my trial. Could I just show you what I thought I might do on the witness stand?

BILLY. Go ahead.

VELMA. Hit it!

([MUSIC] as **ENSEMBLE MEN** *enter.)*

[SONG: No. 25 – "WHEN VELMA TAKES THE STAND"]

VELMA. Well, when I got on the stand, I thought I'd take a peek at the jury, and then I'd cross my legs like this.

ENSEMBLE MEN.
WHEN VELMA TAKES THE STAND.

VELMA. Then, when Harrison cross examines me, I thought I'd give 'em this...and then if he yells at me I thought I'd tremble like this..."Ooo, no, please stop!"

ENSEMBLE MEN.

WHEN VELMA TAKES THE STAND
LOOK AT LITTLE VEL.
SEE HER GIVE 'EM HELL.
AIN'T SHE DOIN' GRAND?
SHE'S GOT 'EM EATIN' OUT OF THE
PALM OF HER HAND.

VELMA. Then, I thought I'd let it all be too much for me, like real dramatic. Then, I thought I'd get real thirsty and say, "Please, someone, could I have a glass of water?"

ENSEMBLE MEN.

WHEN VELMA TAKES THE STAND.
SEE THAT KELLY GIRL.
MAKE THAT JURY WHIRL.
WHEN SHE TURNS IT ON,
SHE'S GONNA GET 'EM GOIN'
'TIL SHE'S GOT 'EM GONE.

(**ROXIE** *enters.*)

VELMA. Then, I thought I'd cry. Buckets. Only I don't have a handkerchief – and that's when I have to ask you for yours! I really like that part. Don't you? Then, I get up and try to walk, only I'm too weak, so I slump and I slump and I slump and I slump and until finally, I faint!

(**VELMA** *faints.*)

ENSEMBLE MEN.

WHEN SHE ROLLS HER EYES,
WATCH HER TAKE THE PRIZE.
WHEN VELMA TAKES THE STAND.
WHEN VELMA TAKES THE STAND.

(**ENSEMBLE MEN** *exit.*)

ROXIE. Is that really what you're gonna do on the witness stand?

VELMA. Yeah. I thought so.

ROXIE. Can I offer you just the teeniest bit of criticism?

VELMA. Okay!

ROXIE. It stinks!

BILLY. *(to* **VELMA***)* I'll talk to you later.

VELMA. I'm not hurt. I guess I'll go now. But not quietly. May I have my exit music, please?

[SONG: No. 26 – "VELMA TAKES THE STAND EXIT MUSIC"]

ENSEMBLE MEN. (*re-enter*)
WHEN THEY SEE HER SHAKE,
BET SHE TAKES THE CAKE
WHEN VELMA TAKES THE STAND.

(The **ENSEMBLE MEN** *and* **VELMA** *exit.)*

BILLY. I've been waiting for you for ten minutes. Don't do that again. Okay, I got Amos to file for divorce.

ROXIE. Yeah? So now what?

BILLY. So now I can get him on the stand and get him to admit that he made a terrible mistake because he still loves you. And of course, you still love him, and now the jury will be falling all over themselves to play cupid and get you back together again. Smart, huh?

ROXIE. Smart huh.

BILLY. And another thing –

ROXIE. And another thing –

BILLY. When Amos is on the stand, I want you to be knitting. A baby garment!

ROXIE. I don't know how to knit.

BILLY. Then learn.

ROXIE. Listen, I am sick of everybody treating me like some dumb common criminal.

BILLY. But you are some dumb common criminal.

ROXIE. That's better than bein' a greasy lawyer! Who's out for all he can steal!

BILLY. Oh, maybe you could appear in court without me, too. Huh?

ROXIE. Maybe I could...just read the morning papers, Palsie. They love me.

BILLY. Wise up, kid. They'd love you a lot more if you were hanged. You know why? Because it would sell more papers.

ROXIE. You're fired!

BILLY. I quit!

ROXIE. Any lawyer in this town would die to have my case!

BILLY. You're a phony celebrity, kid. In a couple of weeks, nobody'll even know who you are. That's Chicago.

(**BILLY** *exits.*)

ROXIE. Yeah? We'll just see about that!

HUNYAK. No. No. No.

ROXIE. And I want my five grand back, too!

HUNYAK. No. No. No.

Scene Three

(An anteroom in the courthouse.)

MATRON. I'm sorry, Aaron. She still says "no."

AARON. Jesus Christ, don't she know she'll be convicted!

HUNYAK. Uncle Sam jo es igazsagos, o nem fog bortonbe csukni, mert artatlan vagyok.

MATRON. She says Uncle Sam is just and fair and he wouldn't put her in jail because she is innocent. Aaron, I think she's telling the truth.

AARON. What the hell has innocence got to do with it? Look, Mrs. Morton – this is a court appointed thing. I don't get anything from this! Nothing!

MATRON. Whaddya want from me? I've done my best.

HUNYAK. Not…guil…ty.

AARON. Goddam foreign hunky nut.

HUNYAK. Fogok tetszeni Uncle Sam-nek?

MATRON. She says will Uncle Sam like her.

AARON. I don't give a Goddamn what she says unless it's "guilty."

HUNYAK. Not…guil…ty.

*(**BAILIFF** enters.)*

BAILIFF. He's ready for you.

MATRON. Well, here you go.

[MUSIC: No. 27 – "HUNGARIAN HANGING"]

HUNYAK. Not…guil…ty. Not…guil…ty. Not…guil…ty, Uncle Sam.

MATRON. And now, ladies and gentlemen, for your pleasure and your entertainment – we proudly present the one….the only….Katalin Hunyak and her famous Hungarian rope trick.

[MUSIC: Drum roll crescendo]

(**HUNYAK** *exits. Noose drops.*)

[MUSIC: Cymbal crash]

ENSEMBLE MEMBER #1. After 47 years a Cook County precedent has been shattered. Katalin Hunyak was hanged tonight for the brutal axe murder of her husband. The Hungarian woman's last words were, "Not guilty."

Scene Four

(The anteroom of the courthouse. March 9th.)

*(**BILLY** re-enters and joins **ROXIE**, who has seen the hanging.)*

ROXIE. I'm sorry, Billy. I'll do anything you say.

BILLY. Now we're clear about what you're doing on the stand?

ROXIE. I been up all night rehearsing.

BILLY. Alright, let's get to my summation. I'm gonna start with justice and America-blah-blah-blah – then I'll get to your repentance – blah-blah-blah – then I'll say, "If sorrow could avail, Fred Casely would be here now, for she would give her life and gladly, to bring the dead man back." You nod.

ROXIE. That's all?

BILLY. That's all! Then I say – "But we can't do that, gentlemen. You may take her life, but it won't bring Casely back." That's always news to them. And then I go into my final statement, winding up…"We can't give her happiness. But we can give her another chance." And that's all for you.

ROXIE. Like hell it is. It's me they want to see! Not you.

BILLY. It's my speech that brings 'em in and it's my speech that'll save your neck.

ROXIE. Screw you, you Goddamned old crook!

BILLY. Shut up, you dirty little —

*(**BAILIFF** enters.)*

BAILIFF. Mr. Flynn, his honor is here.

BILLY. Thank you. Just a moment.

*(**BAILIFF** exits.)*

BILLY. You ready?

ROXIE. Oh Billy, I'm scared.

*(**ROXIE** exits.)*

BILLY. You got nothing to worry about. It's all a circus, kid. A three-ring circus. These trials – the whole world – all show business. But kid, you're working with a star. The biggest!

[SONG: No. 28 – "RAZZLE DAZZLE"]

GIVE 'EM THE OLD RAZZLE DAZZLE.
RAZZLE DAZZLE 'EM.
GIVE 'EM AN ACT WITH LOTS OF FLASH IN IT
AND THE REACTION WILL BE PASSIONATE.

GIVE 'EM THE OLD HOCUS POCUS.
BEAD AND FEATHER 'EM.
HOW CAN THEY SEE WITH SEQUINS IN THEIR EYES?

WHAT IF YOUR HINGES ALL ARE RUSTING?
WHAT IF, IN FACT, YOU'RE JUST DISGUSTING?

RAZZLE DAZZLE 'EM
AND THEY'LL NEVER CATCH WISE.
GIVE 'EM THE OLD RAZZLE DAZZLE.

ENSEMBLE.

RAZZLE DAZZLE 'EM.

BILLY.

GIVE 'EM A SHOW THAT'S SO SPLENDIFEROUS.
ROW AFTER ROW WILL GROW VOCIFEROUS.

BILLY & ENSEMBLE.

GIVE 'EM THE OLD FLIM FLAM FLUMMOX.

ENSEMBLE.

FOOL AND FRACTURE 'EM.

BILLY.

HOW CAN THEY HEAR THE TRUTH ABOVE THE ROAR?

ENSEMBLE. *(growled)*

ROAR!
ROAR!
ROAR!

THROW 'EM A FAKE AND A FINAGLE.
THEY'LL NEVER KNOW, YOU'RE JUST

BILLY.

A BAGEL.
RAZZLE DAZZLE 'EM

BILLY & ENSEMBLE.

AND THEY'LL BEG YOU FOR MORE.

ENSEMBLE. *(sinister laughs, two times)*

(whispered)

GIVE 'EM THE OLD RAZZLE DAZZLE.

RAZZLE DAZZLE 'EM.

BACK SINCE THE DAYS OF OLD METHUSELAH

EVERYONE LOVES THE BIG BAMBOOZ-A-LER.

ENSEMBLE/BILLY (OPTIONAL).

GIVE 'EM THE OLD THREE RING CIRCUS.

STUN AND STAGGER 'EM.

WHEN YOU'RE IN TROUBLE, GO INTO YOUR DANCE.

THOUGH YOU ARE STIFFER THAN A GIRDER,

THEY'LL LET YA GET AWAY

(whispered)

WITH MURDER.

(sung)

RAZZLE DAZZLE 'EM

AND YA GOT A ROMANCE.

BILLY.	**ENSEMBLE.**
GIVE 'EM THE OLD	GIVE 'EM THE OLD
RAZZLE DAZZLE.	RAZZLE DAZZLE.
RAZZLE DAZZLE 'EM.	

BILLY.

GIVE 'EM AN ACT THAT'S UNASSAILABLE,

THEY'LL WAIT A YEAR 'TIL YOU'RE AVAILABLE.

BILLY.	**ENSEMBLE.**
GIVE 'EM THE OLD	GIVE 'EM THE OLD
DOUBLE WHAMMY.	DOUBLE WHAMMY.
DAZE AND DIZZY 'EM.	

BILLY.

SHOW 'EM THE FIRST RATE SORCERER YOU ARE.

ENSEMBLE/BILLY (OPTIONAL).

LONG AS YOU KEEP 'EM WAY OFF BALANCE,

HOW CAN THEY SPOT YA GOT NO TALENTS?

BILLY.

RAZZLE DAZZLE 'EM.

ENSEMBLE.

RAZZLE DAZZLE 'EM.

BILLY.

RAZZLE DAZZLE 'EM.

BILLY & ENSEMBLE.

AND THEY'LL MAKE YOU A STAR.

Scene Five

(The courtroom.)

[MUSIC: No. 29 – "COURTROOM SCENE"]

BILLY. Ladies and gentlemen, we present – Justice.

(The JUDGE pounds his gavel three times.)

JUDGE. The State of Illinois versus Roxie Hart for the murder of Fred Casely.

(Tambourine hit.)

Thank you.

(The JUDGE pounds his gavel once.)

HARRISON. The State calls –

ENSEMBLE. *(in rhythm)* Mr. Amos Hart.

([MUSIC in] as AMOS enters and is sworn in by the CLERK.)

CLERK. Blah, blah, blah, blah, blah, blah, truth, truth, truth. Selp-you God.

AMOS. I certainly do.

HARRISON. Question by Sergeant Fogarty: "What happened next?" Answer by Roxie Hart: "I shot him, because he was walking out on me, the louse."

[MUSIC out]

Signed Roxie Hart. Do you recognize the signature?

AMOS. Yes Sir, it's the signature of the lady who used to be my wife.

HARRISON. Exactly.

[MUSIC: Cymbal choke]

Take the witness.

[MUSIC in]

BILLY. Hello, Amos.

AMOS. Amos, that's right, Mr. Flynn. Amos.

BILLY. Amos, you are at present obtaining a divorce from the defendant? Any reason?

AMOS. I'll say! The newspapers said that she was expecting a little stranger.

BILLY. Well, that's hardly grounds for divorce, is it?

AMOS. A little too much of a stranger.

BILLY. Oh, by that you mean you doubted the paternity of the child.

AMOS. Well, sure!

BILLY. Did you even bother to ask her if you were the father?

AMOS. No sir, but you told me –

BILLY. Just jumped to a conclusion?

[MUSIC: Drum roll]

Do you call that playing square? If Roxie Hart swore that you were the father of her child, which she does –

[MUSIC out]

AMOS. She does?

ROXIE. I do.

BILLY. She does.

[MUSIC: Cymbal choke]

Step down, Daddy.

([MUSIC] as **AMOS** *exits.)*

The defense calls Roxie Hart.

ENSEMBLE. *(in rhythm)* Roxie Hart to the stand.

([MUSIC] as **ROXIE** *takes the stand.)*

CLERK. Blah, blah, blah, blah, blah, blah, truth, truth, truth. Selp-you God.

ROXIE. I do.

[MUSIC: "Roxie"]

ENSEMBLE.
OOOOOOO
OHHHHHH
AHHHHHH

BILLY. What's your name?

ENSEMBLE. *(whispered)* Roxie!

BILLY. Roxie, I have here a statement in which you admit having had illicit relations with the deceased, Fred Casely. Is this statement true or false?

ROXIE. I'm afraid that's true.

BILLY. You're an honest girl, Roxie. When did you first meet Fred Casely?

ROXIE. When he sold Amos and me our furniture. Also he was a regular patron at the nightclub where I was a member of the chorus.

[MUSIC: "Charleston"]

BILLY. And your personal relationship with him – when did that begin?

ROXIE. *(in rhythm)* When I permitted him to drive me home one night.

(FRED enters.)

FRED. Hey, chickie.

ROXIE. Hello, Mr. Casely.

FRED. Fine night for ducks, ain't it? Why don't I drive you home? It's raining so hard and all.

ENSEMBLE. *(whispered)* Charleston…Charleston…Charleston…Charleston.

([MUSIC: Ratchet] as FRED mimes zipping zipper. FRED exits.)

ROXIE. Oh, he seemed like such a fine gentleman.

BILLY. Yet, you were married, Mrs. Hart.

ROXIE. I know. And I don't think I would have gone with him if Mr. Hart and me hadn't quarreled that very morning.

([MUSIC: "Sad Bar Room"] as AMOS enters.)

BILLY. Quarreled? About what?

ROXIE. Oh, Amos, I don't want to work in that cheap Southside nightclub.

AMOS. Yeah, yeah.

ROXIE. And I don't like you working those long hours at the garage either.

AMOS. Sure sure.

ROXIE. Oh Amos, I want a real home and a child.

[MUSIC out]

AMOS. Fat chance.

[MUSIC: Bass drum]

BILLY. So you drifted into this illicit relationship with Fred Casely because you were unhappy at home.

ROXIE. Most unhappy.

AMOS. I love ya, honey. I love ya.

[MUSIC: Bike horn. Drum hits]

BILLY. Yet, you do respect the sacredness of the marriage vow?

ROXIE. Oh yes, sir.

BILLY. Then why didn't you stop this affair with Casely?

ROXIE. I tried to.

(FRED enters.)

But Mr. Casely,

[MUSIC: Clank]

– he'd plead and he'd say –

FRED. I can't live without you! I can't live without you! I can't live without you!

[MUSIC: Pop Gun]

AMOS. I love ya, Honey. I love ya.

[MUSIC: Bike Horn]

ROXIE. I was being torn apart.

([MUSIC: Ratchet. Drum hits] as AMOS and FRED exit.)

BILLY. Roxie Hart, the State has accused you of the murder of Fred Casely. Are you guilty or not guilty?

ROXIE. Not guilty! Not guilty! Oh, I killed him – yes – but I am not a criminal!

BILLY. There, there.

(handing her a handkerchief)

There, there.

(Thrusts the handkerchief toward her. **ROXIE** *remembers to sob.)*

ENSEMBLE. *(continues under the scene)*

GIVE 'EM THE OLD RAZZLE DAZZLE.

RAZZLE DAZZLE THEM.

BACK SINCE THE DAYS OF OLD MATHUSALEH,

EV'RYONE LOVES THE BIG BAMBOOZ-A-LER.

GIVE 'EM THE OLD THREE RING CIRCUS,

STUN AND STAGGER 'EM.

WHEN YOU'RE IN TROUBLE...

BILLY. Roxie, can you recall the night of February 14th?

ROXIE. Yes sir.

BILLY. Tell the Jury, in your own way, the happenings of that night.

ROXIE. Well, it was after work about 2 a.m. and I stopped in at an all night grocery store to pick up some baking powder to make cup cakes for my Amos. Oh, Amos just loved my cup cakes. And then, I went right home. And I was getting ready for bed when, suddenly the doorbell rang.

ENSEMBLE.

"DING-DONG".

[MUSIC out. Doorbell]

Now, I thought it was my girlfriend, Gloria, so I slipped into my kimono and went to the door.

[MUSIC: Tremolo]

BILLY. And who was there?

[MUSIC: Chord]

ROXIE. Fred Casely.

BILLY. And what did he say, Roxie?

FRED. That note you wrote me! Telling me it was all over? Why did you write it!

ROXIE. Because I have seen the error of my ways and…

BILLY. And?

(**ROXIE** *forgets her story.*)

ROXIE. And?

BILLY. And?

ROXIE. And?

BILLY. And when you asked him to, did he go away?

HARRISON. I object! The counsel is leading the witness.

JUDGE. Sustained!

(**JUDGE** *hits gavel once.*)

BILLY. I'll rephrase the question. What did you say?

ROXIE. I said, "Go away!"

ENSEMBLE. Beat it, buddy.

(**JUDGE** *hits gavel three times.*)

ROXIE. I tried to close the door, but he forced his way in. I ran into the bedroom,

[*MUSIC: Three beats*]

…but he followed me.

[*MUSIC: Four beats*]

FRED. Look, just have one little drink with me and I'll go.

BILLY. Why didn't you scream?

ROXIE. I was afraid to wake the neighbors.

[*MUSIC: Tremolo*]

(*to* **FRED**) Please, no good will come of this, and besides, I love my husband.

ENSEMBLE.
HALLELUJAH!
HALLELUJAH!
HALLELUJAH!

BILLY. So you told him that you loved your husband and what did he say to that?

FRED. It doesn't matter.

(**JUDGE** *claps on each "mine."*)

You're mine. You're mine. You're mine.

[*MUSIC: Apache*]

(**ENSEMBLE**: *seven fast handclaps.*)

ROXIE. I can't go on. I can't go on. I can't go on.

BILLY. No, Roxie, you must tell the Jury everything. They have a right to know.

ROXIE. Okay.

(**ROXIE** *taps* **FRED**'s *shoulder.*)

[*MUSIC: Woodblock three times*]

(*To* **FRED**:) Amos and me are going to have a baby.

[*MUSIC: Cymbal choke*]

BILLY. And what did he say to that?

FRED. I'll kill you before I see you have another man's child!

[*MUSIC: Rim shot*]

BILLY. What happened next?

[*MUSIC: Tremolo*]

ROXIE. In his passion he ripped off my kimono and threw me across the room! (*to a* **JUROR** *who has pinched her:*) Oh, you nasty man! (*continuing*) Mr. Hart's revolver was layin' there between us. He grabbed for the gun –

[*MUSIC: Chord*]

I knocked it from his hand –

[*MUSIC: Chord*]

he whirled me aside.

[*MUSIC: Sustained chord*]

ROXIE. (*to the* **JUROR** *who pinches her again*) Will you cut that out?

BILLY. And then?

ROXIE. And then, *(in rhythm)* we both reached for the gun.

> *[MUSIC: Chord]*

> But I got it first.

ENSEMBLE. Hurray!

> *[MUSIC: Tremolo]*

ROXIE. Then, he came toward me with that funny look in his eyes.

FRED. I mean to kill you!

BILLY. Did you think he meant to kill you?

ROXIE. Oh, yes, sir.

BILLY. So it was his life or yours?

> *[MUSIC: Chord]*

ROXIE. And not just mine! **(ROXIE** *pats her stomach two times with music.)*

> *[MUSIC: Two bass drum hits. Violin baby cry]*

> So I closed my eyes and I shot!

> *[MUSIC: Rim shot]*

FRED CASELY. Roxie –

> *[MUSIC: Rim shot]*

> Roxie, please –

> *[MUSIC: Rim shot]*

ENSEMBLE. *(whispered)* Hey!

BILLY. In defense of your life!

ENSEMBLE.

> RAZZLE DAZZLE 'EM.
> RAZZLE DAZZLE

ROXIE. To save my husband's unborn child!

ENSEMBLE.

> AND THEY'LL MAKE YOU A STAR!

> **(JUDGE** *hits gavel two times.)*

Scene Six

(The jail.)

[MUSIC: No. 30 – NBC CHIMES]

MARY SUNSHINE. *(as if she were reporting from the courtroom over the radio.)* Mrs. Hart's behavior throughout this ordeal has been truly extraordinary!

VELMA. I bet it has.

MARY SUNSHINE. Seated next to her attorney, Mr. Billy Flynn, she weeps! But she fishes in her handbag and cannot find a handkerchief!

VELMA. Handkerchief?

MARY SUNSHINE. Finally, her attorney, Mr. Flynn, hands her one!

VELMA. That's my bit.

MATRON. Shhh, I wanna hear.

MARY SUNSHINE. The poor child has had no relief. She looks around now, bewildered seeming to want something. Oh, it's a glass of water. The bailiff has brought her one.

VELMA. A glass of water! That's mine too!

MARY SUNSHINE. Mrs. Hart, her usual gracious self, thanks the bailiff and he smiles at her. She looks simply radiant in her stylish blue lace dress and elegant silver shoes.

VELMA. With rhinestone buckles?

MARY SUNSHINE. With rhinestone buckles.

VELMA. Aaahhh!!

MATRON. Velma, take it easy!

VELMA. But those were my shoes and she stole 'em!

MATRON. Well, you shouldn't have left them layin' around.

VELMA. First she steals my publicity, my lawyer, my trial date, and now my shoes!

MATRON. Well, whaddya expect? She's a lowbrow. The whole world's gone lowbrow. Things ain't what they used to be.

[SONG: No. 31 – "CLASS"]

VELMA. They sure ain't, Mama. It's all gone.

WHATEVER HAPPENED TO FAIR DEALING,
AND PURE ETHICS,
AND NICE MANNERS?
WHY IS IT EVERYONE NOW
IS A PAIN IN THE ASS?
WHATEVER HAPPENED TO CLASS?

MATRON.

CLASS
WHATEVER HAPPENED TO, "PLEASE, MAY I"?
AND, "YES, THANK YOU",
AND, "HOW CHARMING"?
NOW, EVERY SON OF A BITCH
IS A SNAKE IN THE GRASS.
WHATEVER HAPPENED TO CLASS?

VELMA.

CLASS!

VELMA AND MATRON.

AH, THERE AIN'T NO GENTLEMEN
TO OPEN UP THE DOORS.
THERE AIN'T NO LADIES NOW,
THERE'S ONLY PIGS AND WHORES.
AND EVEN KIDS'LL KNOCK YA DOWN
SO'S THEY CAN PASS,
NOBODY'S GOT NO CLASS.

VELMA.

WHATEVER HAPPENED TO OLD VALUES

MATRON.

AND FINE MORALS

VELMA.

AND GOOD BREEDING?

MATRON.

NOW, NO ONE EVEN SAYS "OOPS"
WHEN THEY'RE PASSING THEIR GAS.

VELMA & MATRON.

WHATEVER HAPPENED TO CLASS?
CLASS

VELMA & MATRON. *(cont.)*

> AH, THERE AIN'T NO GENTLEMEN
> THAT'S FIT FOR ANY USE.
> AND ANY GIRL'D TOUCH YOUR PRIVATES
> FOR A DEUCE.

MATRON.

> AND EVEN KIDS'LL KICK YOUR SHINS
> AND GIVE YOU SASS.

VELMA.

> AND EVEN KIDS'LL KICK YOUR SHINS
> AND GIVE YOU SASS.

VELMA & MATRON.

> NOBODY'S GOT NO CLASS.

VELMA.

> ALL YOU READ ABOUT TODAY IS RAPE AND THEFT.

MATRON.

> JESUS CHRIST!
> AIN'T THERE NO DECENCY LEFT?

VELMA & MATRON.

> NOBODY'S GOT NO CLASS!

MATRON.

> EVERYBODY YOU WATCH

VELMA.

> 'S GOT HIS BRAINS IN HIS CROTCH.

MATRON.

> HOLY CRAP!

VELMA.

> HOLY CRAP!

MATRON.

> WHAT A SHAME.

VELMA.

> WHAT A SHAME.

VELMA & MATRON.

> WHAT BECAME OF CLASS?

Scene 7

(The courtroom.)

[MUSIC: No. 32 – "BILLY'S SPEECH"]

[MUSIC: Drum roll]

MARY SUNSHINE. Ladies and Gentlemen, the final day of the trial of Roxie Hart has come. A hush has fallen over the courtroom as Billy Flynn prepares his summation to the jury. The next voice you hear will be that of Mr. Flynn –

[MUSIC: Drum roll stops]

– champion of the downtrodden.

[MUSIC in]

BILLY. Ladies and Gentlemen, you and I have never killed. We can't know the agony, the hell that Roxie Hart lived through then. This drunken beast, Fred Casely, forced his way into her home, forced liquor upon her, physically abused her, and threatened her life. At that moment, motherly love and a deep concern for her neighbors stirred within her. She shot him. We don't deny that. But she has prayed to God for forgiveness for what she has done. Yes, you may take her life, but it won't bring Casely back. Look, look closely at that frail figure. My God, hasn't she been punished enough? We can't give her happiness, but we can give her another chance. You have heard my colleague call her temptress, call her adulteress, call her murderess. But, despite what the Prosecution says, things are not always what they appear to be.

MARY SUNSHINE. *(vocal ad lib)*

AHHH

*(**BILLY** removes **MARY SUNSHINE**'s jacket and wig to reveal her to be a him.)*

BILLY. The defense rests!

*(**MARY SUNSHINE** exits.)*

Scene Eight

(The courtroom.)

JUDGE. Order! Order! I said order! Members of the Jury. Have you reached a verdict?

JUROR. We have, your Honor.

JUDGE. Will the defendant please rise? And what is your verdict?

JUROR. We find the defendant –

[MUSIC: No. 33 – "THE VERDICT"]

[MUSIC: Percussion gunshots]

(Enormous confusion. A REPORTER rushes in.)

ENSEMBLE MEMBER #1. You should see what's going on out there! There was this divorce action and this babe shot her husband, his mother, and the defense attorney. There is blood all over the walls. It's terrible. But what a story!

(Everyone exits. There's pandemonium. BILLY and ROXIE remain.)

ROXIE. I'm Roxie Hart! Don't you want my picture? What the hell happened?

BILLY. You were found not guilty, that's what happened.

ROXIE. Who the hell cares about that?

BILLY. I saved your life.

ROXIE. Where are all the photographers – the reporters? The publicity? I was countin' on that.

BILLY. You know, your gratitude is overwhelming. But forget it, I'm only in it for the money anyway.

ROXIE. Yeah, you get five thousand dollars and I wind up with nothin'.

BILLY. You're a free woman, Roxie Hart, and God save Illinois! My exit music please.

[MUSIC in]

BILLY/ENSEMBLE WOMEN.

ALL I (HE) CARE(S) ABOUT IS LOVE.

(BILLY/ENSEMBLE WOMEN exit. AMOS enters.)

AMOS. Roxie?

ROXIE. What do you want?

AMOS. I'd like you to come home. You said you still wanted me. I still love you. And the baby. Our baby....

ROXIE. Baby? Jesus, what do you take me for? There ain't no baby!

AMOS. There ain't no baby?

ROXIE. That's right.

AMOS. Roxie, I still love you.

ROXIE. They didn't even want my picture. I don't understand that. They didn't even want my picture.

AMOS. My exit music, please...

[MUSIC: the ORCHESTRA doesn't play]

...Okay.

(AMOS exits.)

ROXIE. ...gone...

[MUSIC: No. 34 – "NOWADAYS"]

...all gone.

IT'S GOOD, ISN'T IT?
GRAND, ISN'T IT?
GREAT, ISN'T IT?
SWELL, ISN'T IT?
FUN, ISN'T IT?
NOWADAYS.

THERE'S MEN EVERYWHERE,
JAZZ EVERYWHERE,
BOOZE EVERYWHERE,
LIFE EVERYWHERE,
JOY EVERYWHERE,
NOWADAYS.

ROXIE. *(cont.)*

> YOU CAN LIKE THE LIFE YOU'RE LIVIN'.
> YOU CAN LIVE THE LIFE YOU LIKE.
> YOU CAN EVEN MARRY HARRY,
> BUT MESS AROUND WITH IKE.
>
> AND THAT'S
> GOOD, ISN'T IT?
> GRAND, ISN'T IT?
> GREAT, ISN'T IT?
> SWELL.

*(**ROXIE** exits.)*

ENSEMBLE MEMBER #2. Ladies and Gentlemen, the McVickers Theatre, Chicago's finest home of family entertainment, is proud to announce a first. The first time, anywhere, there has been an act of this nature. Not only one little lady but two! You've read about them in the papers and now here they are – a double header! Chicago's own killer dillers – those two scintillating sinners – Roxie Hart and Velma Kelly!

*(**ROXIE** and **VELMA** enter during speech.)*

ROXIE & VELMA.

> YOU CAN LIKE THE LIFE YOU'RE LIVIN'.
> YOU CAN LIVE THE LIFE YOU LIKE.
> YOU CAN EVEN MARRY HARRY,
> BUT MESS AROUND WITH IKE.
>
> AND THAT'S
> GOOD, ISN'T IT?
> GRAND, ISN'T IT?
> GREAT, ISN'T IT?
> SWELL, ISN'T IT?
> FUN, ISN'T IT?
> BUT NOTHIN' STAYS.
>
> IN FIFTY YEARS OR SO,
> IT'S GONNA CHANGE, YOU KNOW,
> BUT, OH, IT'S HEAVEN,
> NOWADAYS.

([DANCE] ROXIE *and* VELMA *are "poetry in motion, two moving as one.")*

[MUSIC: ENSEMBLE *member whistles]*

ROXIE AND VELMA. *(breathy)*

WA WA
WA, WA, WA, WA, WA
WA WA,
WA, WA, WA, WA WA
WA WA,
WA, WA, WA, WA WA

AND THAT'S
GOOD, ISN'T IT?
GRAND, ISN'T IT?
GREAT, ISN'T IT?
SWELL, ISN'T IT?
FUN, ISN'T IT?
BUT NOTHIN' STAYS.

IN FIFTY YEARS OR SO,
IT'S GONNA CHANGE, YOU KNOW,
BUT, OH, IT'S HEAVEN,
NOWADAYS.

[MUSIC: No. 35 – "HOT HONEY RAG"]

MARY SUNSHINE. *(as a man.)* Okay, you babes of jazz. Let's pick up the pace. Let's shake the blues away. Let's make the parties longer. Let's make the skirts shorter and shorter. Let's make the music hotter. Let's all go to hell in a fast car and KEEP IT HOT!

(dance)

[MUSIC: No. 36 – "FINALE"]

VELMA/ROXIE. *(Repeat "thank yous." Ad-lib. MUSIC in.)*

VELMA. Roxie and I would just like to take this opportunity to thank you – for your faith and your belief in our innocence.

ROXIE. It was your letters, telegrams, and words of encouragement that helped see us through our terrible ordeal.

VELMA. You know, a lot of people have lost faith in America.

ROXIE. And for what America stands for.

VELMA. But we are the living examples of what a wonderful country this is.

[MUSIC changes to "ALL THAT JAZZ"]

ROXIE. So we'd just like to say thank you and God bless you.

VELMA/ROXIE.	**ENSEMBLE.**
God Bless you. Thank you and God bless you....God be with you. God walk with you always. God bless you. God bless you.	NO, I'M NO ONE'S WIFE, BUT, OH, I LOVE MY LIFE AND ALL THAT JAZZ!
	(loud whisper)
	THAT JAZZ!

(Curtain)

[MUSIC: No. 37 – "BOWS"]

[MUSIC: No. 38 – "EXIT MUSIC"]

CPSIA information can be obtained
at www.ICGtesting.com
Printed in the USA
LVOW01s1414250816
501854LV00046B/518/P